AN AMISH CHRISTMAS BLESSING

FIVE AMISH BROTHERS

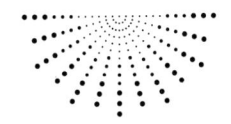

SARAH MILLER

SWEETBOOKHUB.COM

FIVE AMISH BROTHERS

Welcome to the third of 5 books about 5 Amish brothers.

Like most families, our brothers love each other. They are also, very different people, with different hopes and dreams. When they lose their *daed*, and the harsh reality of their future is revealed can they pull together to find love and a secure future, or will it pull them apart?

Join them and the residents of Faith's Creek as they grow into men their *daed* would be proud of.

Blessings,

Sarah Miller

Join my newsletter for accessional free content and to be the first to find out about new books.

If you missed the first books you can grab them here, all are FREE on KU

A Love to Heal her Heart

A Love so Bright

CHAPTER ONE

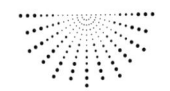

"Stop looking out of the window, it won't change things," Ester Phillips said as she eased her weight down onto the bed as gently as she could. It was not the most dignified or comfortable of descents, but she didn't mind. This was her friend's wedding day and they were going to celebrate.

Only, Leah Chandler, couldn't pull her eyes away from the falling snow and the constant stream of buggies pulling into the farm. It was so exciting. Everything she wanted. "I know it is silly, but being married, being part of a family in time for Christmas. I can't tell you how much it means to me." Turning, she noticed that Ester was sitting on the bed and holding her rather large stomach.

"It isn't silly at all," Ester said.

Leah felt a spike of panic send jitters into her stomach and raise goosebumps on her arms. "Are you all right?" *Could the boppli be coming this early?*

Ester waved her hands in front of her face and shook her head. "I'm fine, I'm not ill, I'm just pregnant." Giving her friend a smile, Ester patted her belly. "This one can just be a little heavy at times. I never knew what backache was, until I hit six months."

Leah came across to the bed and took her friend's hands in hers. "I am so excited for you. Do you think it will be a boy or a girl?"

Ester chuckled. "The only thing I pray for is an easy labor. But don't tell Jeremiah. He wants a son."

"And what about you, really?" Leah was excited for the upcoming wedding but the thought of her best friend having a *boppli*, that thrilled her almost as much. She closed her eyes and thought of the joy, how would she feel when it was her turn? Happiness was like a cloak that covered her with its warmth.

"I don't know," Ester said. "Some days, I dream about baking with my daughter and all the things we will talk about. Others, I can't wait to help my son grow into a man." She chuckled. "It doesn't matter, I will have lots of *kinner*, I know it."

Leah sat on the bed next to her and chuckled too. "I can't wait to have a house full. All the joy and laughter, all the questions and silly things that *kinner* say. Having them grow up with your *kinner,* too. It is so exciting. I'm not looking forward to washing all the diapers, though."

"With joy comes work and with work comes joy." Ester chuckled. "You would hate it if you had nothing to do."

"And so would you." Leah stood and looked at her friend for long moments.

"What is it? You're making me nervous, and, you really should be getting ready. If you don't go downstairs soon, Abraham will think you have abandoned him."

"*Nee*, he won't." Tears were forming in Leah's eyes and she wiped them away and blinked rapidly. "I was just thinking how far we had both come. If you remember, when Rhonda passed, we thought you would be lonely, a spinster for life, and that I would be searching for somewhere to live. Here you are, married, and soon to have your first *boppli*. When once you were... shy around so many people... well, all people... now you have so many friends."

"Never around you," Ester said but her cheeks were blushing a little.

"You have been a *gut* friend to me, and to see how far you have come, it fills me with joy. Today is so happy, I could burst."

Ester stood and pulled her friend into a hug. "Careful, or we will both be crying. We do not want tears and red eyes to spoil your pretty face and your wedding day, now do we?"

Leah leaned into the hug and squeezed her friend tightly. "It might be hard to stop them, but I will do my best. It is so wonderful that you will now be my sister-in-law."

"And I am so pleased that you will be an aunt to my little bundle of kicks," Ester said.

"That is an unusual name." Leah chuckled.

"But the most appropriate one, I can assure you. Now, let's get you ready."

"I think I am." Leah took a step back and looked at herself in the mirror. Though her friend called her pretty, she had always thought she was... well, as a *kinner* she had been teased and called a freak. The taunts still hurt her, and she found it hard to find anything pleasing about her reflection.

Staring back at her, from beneath her *kapp*, was a pair of violet eyes and a face so pale it looked like she had never seen the sun. Dr. Yoder had told her that her unusual eye color was because she had a condition called albinism. It meant that she had very little pigment in her skin. It had meant a lonely *kinnerhood* and when her folks died she lived wherever she could, currently with her friend, Dinah and Conrad, her *daed*. A man who was not too well.

Ester had a similar lonely *kinnerhood*, it was her shyness after her folks passed that had been her problem. Though her aunt took *gut* care of her, Ester was withdrawn for a long time.

The two of them had come together. They were teased and outcasts and had become *gut* friends because of it. Ester had never been comfortable around men and had spent many years looking after her aunt. For Leah, courtship was also rare, if she was honest, non-existent. The men did not wish to pass this condition on to their *kinner*. Shock almost dropped her to her knees. Would she? Would they have this awful pale skin, these strangely colored eyes, would they be taunted as she had been?

"Stop it," Ester said. "You are catastrophizing and thinking too much."

"Sorry." Leah closed her eyes and opened them once more. She didn't look too bad. The royal blue dress that she and Ester had made, was exactly the same style as her everyday dress, but it looked... different. It suited her coloring and toned down her eyes. She had to admit it was wonderful and it made her smile. She did not think that *Gott* would resent her a little pride on this day.

From now on, she could wear a black apron to the fortnightly service. It would tell the whole district that she was married. That she was no longer Chandler but now Phillips. Of course, they would all know, for they were all coming to her wedding. The joy was so much that she wanted to shout it from the rooftops.

But what about her *kinner*, were they to be a freak like her? Dr. Yoder had told her it was unlikely. Her parents had been from another district. He had mentioned something about genes and that both parents had to carry the gene for the child to get this condition. In his mind, as no one from their district had this condition, it was almost impossible for her to pass it on. It made no sense, her parents had both looked normal.

"Stop it, you are thinking again." Ester took her hands and squeezed them gently. "I understand your fear about *boppli's* but you have to believe in the doctor and trust *Gott*. Enjoy this day, enjoy what comes, and face the challenges with prayer and a *gut* heart and you will be fine. Abraham loves you, we all love you, that is all that matters.

Leah wiped away her tears and pulled her friend into a hug. She was right, today was not a day for worry. It was a day for a wedding and a celebration, but did Abraham worry as she did, would it pull them apart?

CHAPTER TWO

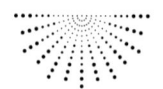

Leah stood in the Phillips' barn in front of Bishop Amos Beiler, Abraham Phillips, and the whole of the Faith's Creek district. Excitement and joy coursed through her veins making her feel so alive. She had hardly heard a word of the ceremony and her voice had almost failed her. As the snow fell outside, it felt cozy and homely in the barn. There were no draughts, and it was filled with love and a sense of celebration.

Now, overcome with joy, she felt tears slide down her face, as Amos announced them husband and *fraa*.

They walked together between their family and friends, receiving congratulations and best wishes.

"You look so beautiful and I am so proud of you," Dinah Gunden said as Leah stopped at her side.

Leah pulled her in for a hug. Dinah and her *daed* had looked after her for so long now, but she was finally leaving them. "I wish you the happiness I feel."

"*Denke*," Dinah said as tears slipped down her face.

Leah knew that Dinah believed she would never marry, her life was taken up with caring for her *daed*, but Leah also knew, that *Gott* would find a way.

While Leah and her new husband spoke with well-wishers, the barn would be converted for the celebratory meal. It was something that was done at every wedding and the district was well-versed in the procedure. The transformation would be quicker than she could imagine.

"Congratulations, and enjoy your new life, we will miss you but we wish you well," Dinah said.

"*Denke*, you know that I will always be grateful for my time with you?" Leah replied.

Dinah was such a beautiful girl with her brown hair peeking from beneath her *kapp* and her all too serious dark brown eyes. But the seventeen-year-old always had a ready smile, despite her hard life.

"You have nothing to be grateful for; *Daed* and I will miss you."

As more people crowded around Leah, she had to move on. "We will speak soon," she said as Dinah was left alone.

* * *

Dinah sighed, it had been such a lovely wedding and she was not lying when she said she would miss Leah. Though she loved her *daed* and her life, it would be a little lonelier without Leah living with them. It would also be a little harder, though she took in a bit of mending, Dinah and Conrad had very little income.

"When will you be married?" Jeremiah Phillips asked Dinah, jerking her out of her thoughts.

Though she knew he was trying to be nice, the words cut her to her core. Heat flooded her cheeks and she tried to turn away. It was not likely that she would ever marry. Looking after her *daed* left no time for courtship. "Not for a while," she said, knowing that this was just polite conversation and not really a chance for a discussion.

"You would make someone a fine *fraa*," Jeremiah said but his eyes were drawn to Ester. His own *fraa* was glowing with her pregnancy and Jeremiah smiled once more before nodding to Dinah and making his way to Ester.

Dinah did not mean to feel lonely, she shouldn't have, standing there amongst all her friends and district members, but she did. Leah was smiling and talking to the next to youngest of the Phillip's brothers. It looked like he was welcoming her into the family with a big smile beneath his unruly red hair.

Dinah knew he had flashing green eyes and a ready smile. If she were ever to court, a man like Uri Phillips would be her preference. She chuckled and pulled her eyes away before he caught her staring. That was never going to happen. A man like Uri could have his pick of women and he wouldn't choose one that never ventured out of the house for anything other than service, weddings, and shopping.

Uri turned before she could remove her stare and caught her eye. He smiled, and Dinah felt her heart leap a little. Then she looked around, for she was sure he must have been smiling at someone else. There was no one behind her but when she looked back Uri had gone.

Dinah moved around the barn, looking for a seat. She wanted to find one with people she knew. That sounded ridiculous, for she knew everyone here, but many of them she had never spoken to.

"Did you enjoy the wedding?"

Dinah turned at the sound of the man's voice and found herself looking straight into the clear green eyes of Uri. Once more, she checked around to see if he was talking to someone else, but there was no one close enough or looking in their direction. "I did, *denke*." She knew that her voice shook and that her cheeks were burning and she lowered her head to look at her hands.

"I did too, Leah will be a great addition to our family," Uri said, his own words were a little stiff. As if he was struggling to make small talk.

Dinah wanted to tell him that he didn't have to talk to her but she couldn't get the words out. She looked up and he was smiling. It was such a lovely smile that she started to relax.

"I... err... I," Uri shrugged his shoulders, his own face was bright red and he lowered his head."

Dinah thought he would turn and run. What was wrong with her? Was she so scary that men ran from her? At that moment, Colin Phillips slapped his brother on the back.

"How are you, Dinah, and how is Conrad?" Colin asked with easy confidence.

Dinah did not know him well as he had left on his *rumspringa* and stayed away for a number of years. There had been rumors that he would never return, but he did, shortly after his *daed* passed.

"*Denke* for asking," Dinah said. "I am *gut* and my *daed*, he has *gut* days and bad days. Today was a *gut* one and he was so pleased that I could attend the wedding. It has been a lovely ceremony; your family is growing quickly."

"*Ack*, it is. I'm only just back myself and already we have two new women." Colin shook his head and made an expression of mock horror. "Trust me, the food is much better." Colin winked. "I know that we are all pleased you could make it," Colin said and he elbowed Uri. "Some, I think, more than others."

Uri coughed and looked down, his cheeks still glowing as red as his hair. "It is nice to see you," Uri said. "Hopefully, if Conrad improves, we will see more of you."

Dinah smiled, feeling her heart leap with joy. "I would like that."

"Dinah, come sit here," Ester called, she was sitting close to the Eck; the place of honor for the happy couple.

Leah turned back to the two men but Uri could not hold her gaze. He dropped his eyes and fiddled with his hands, twisting them together as if in stress.

"Go," Colin said. "Wish Conrad well from us all."

"I will." Dinah left the two brothers and as she walked away they went into a mock fight. Colin grabbed Uri and rubbed his head as he pulled him into a bear hug. Dinah felt a little letdown, she had thought that Uri was interested in seeing her, but perhaps, he was just inquiring about her father, being polite. And Colin, like all brothers, was teasing him, trying to embarrass him.

It didn't matter, she would enjoy the wedding; after all, she had never expected romance in her life. This was a chance to socialize and she didn't get many of them, she would make the most of it.

* * *

Uri watched Dinah walk away and cursed his own tongue for being so thick and unwieldy in his mouth whenever she was around. There was Colin, who had been away for so long, who some still treated as an

Englischer, and yet he spoke eloquently and confidently. Whereas Uri had stood there like a bumbling idiot.

What must she think of me?

Maybe that he was a fool or worse, that he was rude. Why hadn't he asked about her *daed*? It was such a simple thing, an expected thing, and yet, when he saw her, all he thought about was her and his mind turned to mush.

As he watched her laughing and talking with Ester and Jeremiah he hoped that he would see more of her and that when he did, he hoped he would be able to form a complete sentence, preferably, one that made sense.

CHAPTER THREE

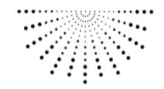

Dinah took a seat next to the fire and smiled across at her *daed* before she picked up a dress that needed mending. The seam had split, it was old and the material was worn. She had already completed a bag of mending for Mary Byler and her fingers were sore, but she would finish this dress of her own before she stopped.

"You are always working," Conrad said.

"*Ack, Daed*, it is just a touch of mending." Dinah smiled. "Do you need anything?"

"*Nee*, I have everything I could ask for. I wish I wasn't such a burden."

"You are not." Dinah lifted her head so quickly and her eyes flashed. She hated it when he thought this. "Never, I love being here with you and what else would I do?"

"Well, maybe you should start courting." He chuckled. "You need young people in your life. Now Leah has gone I worry for you."

Dinah looked across at her *daed*, he did look stronger today but he sat in the wheelchair with a worn blanket over his knees, *she must do something about that*, and a cup of coffee, and his Bible at his side. If she were not here, what would he do? What if he slipped or needed something. *Nee*, it was too worrying to think about. This was the life *Gott* has given her and she was grateful.

"I will think about it," Dinah said. "But today, I need to mend this dress, or I will likely burst a seam when I'm reaching up to hang the washing. What would happen then? I know what, Alima Byler would report me to the bishop for lewd behavior."

"Lewd, she would at that." He chuckled. "Maybe, you should buy some new material and make a new dress?" Conrad said as he ran a hand through his silver hair.

"Maybe, but not today." Dinah took a sip of her own coffee. It was warm and strong and gave her the strength to keep smiling. Though she wanted to court, it was not to be. Though she wanted to buy new material, there was no money for it. Perhaps she could barter for some of the jelly she had made. It had been a *gut* year for blackberries and she had picked many from the hedgerow.

"Tell me about the wedding again," Conrad asked.

Dinah smiled, reliving the memories made her feel a little less lonely. "Oh, it was glorious. Leah was so beautiful, her cheeks glowing red as she made her way to Abraham and Bishop Beiler."

Conrad's face lit up as she told him of the wedding and of all their friends and neighbors. It did her *gut* to see a light in his eyes and to hope that this connection would help him recover. Dr. Yoder had told them that he may recover in time, but that it was down to *Gott's* will.

"How I would love to attend your wedding one day," Conrad said but the words were broken by a fit of coughing.

"*Ack, Daed*, don't get excited." Dinah fetched his medicine and gave him a spoonful. It eased the coughing but she could see that he was pale. "Why don't I take you back to your room, you can lie down for an hour?"

"I don't want to be any trouble," he said.

Dinah shook her head. "You are never trouble, *Daed*. Come." She wheeled him through to the bedroom and helped him out of the chair and onto the bed. With a huge pile of cushions, so he was comfortable but upright, she tucked a blanket over him. Already, his eyes were closing and she hoped that he would sleep for an hour or two, while he did she would pray for him.

Dinah, took one last look at him before leaving the room and returning to the mending. As she did, her mind flicked back to the wedding and the encounter with Uri and Colin Phillips. Both of the brothers were fine men. Shaking her head, she chuckled to herself. It was foolish to imagine that anything could happen between them. But, she may as well enjoy her imagination, and dreaming never hurt.

Of the two men, she felt a pull in Uri's direction. He was handsome and sweet and there was something about him, but Colin seemed to like her more. Could there ever be a chance for her, a chance for love and marriage? Closing her eyes, she imagined walking through the Phillips' barn to meet her new husband. It was a glorious dream, but just that. Now, it was time to see if she could make this dress last a little longer.

* * *

Colin finished milking the cows and placed the milk in the pantry. What should he do now? He was still trying to make amends with his brothers for abandoning them after his *rumspringa*. No one seemed to mention it anymore, and they seemed to have accepted him as part of the family, but he still felt guilty. He wanted to find ways to make up for it.

As he came out of the house he saw Uri sitting on the bench under the tree. It was snowing and cold, what was his brother doing? Then it struck him, was his brother in love?

Colin went to the kitchen and made 2 cups of coffee before making his way over to Uri. "It's too chilly to be out here, I thought you might like this?"

Uri looked up, his face was slack and the blue smudges beneath his eyes, made it look like he had not been sleeping. "*Denke*, that is kind."

"What is wrong, little brother?" Colin handed him the cup and took a seat. The bench was cold, it would be much nicer to have this conversation by a roaring fire but he would take it easy. Uri might not be ready to admit his feelings, just yet.

Uri shrugged and sipped the coffee but said nothing.

"I really enjoyed the wedding," Colin said. "Leah is so nice and her friend, Dinah… she seems nice too."

Uri looked up at the mention of Dinah, and Colin had his suspicions confirmed. "Do you find her interesting?" Colin asked.

Uri dropped his head, his cheeks glowing red. "I do, but I am so… useless when it comes to women. I'm a clutz. I open my mouth and rubbish comes out… if anything at all. Often, I just stare, as if I have nothing but wool between my ears."

"I'm sure it is not that bad," Colin said with a chuckle, even though he could see it was.

"It is, you spoke to her confidently and eloquently… I just burbled."

Colin chuckled again and slapped his brother on the back. "Then we shall have to find a way to help."

"How?" Uri asked and there was a look of hope in his eyes.

"Leave it with me, I will find a way. In the meantime, pray on it. Maybe *Gott* will offer some suggestions."

Uri dropped his head with disappointment and Colin felt his own wave of disappointment.

"I will help you, I promise," he said, even though for now, he had no idea how to do so. After all, he hardly knew Dinah so how could he bring the two of them together?

CHAPTER FOUR

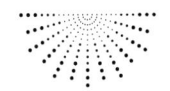

Colin decided he needed a little help; after all, he hardly knew Dinah and didn't remember her *daed* at all. Jeremiah would have been the logical brother to speak to. As the eldest, and most settled of the brothers, he was well respected and known by almost everyone in the district. However, there was still tension between the two of them.

Colin regretted this and knew it was his own fault. He had put his own happiness above that of the family, look how *gut* that had worked out! Maybe, by doing this he could help his brother see that he was back for *gut*. That he put the family first, but how could he help Uri?

Abraham was also very steady and well respected but Colin knew that he was newly married and had plenty on his hands. For some reason, Moses came to mind when he thought of helping Uri out. The two brothers would do something *gut* for Uri, at the same time, Colin would work on building his brother's confidence. After all, Uri was great with the customers of their small holding. He had done much to help in their current success.

As Colin sought Moses out, he knew that this would be easy. Seeing Uri happy and married would fill him with joy. As big flakes of snow fluttered down and the talk was of Christmas and celebration, Colin looked for Moses.

* * *

"What is up with Colin?" Betsy Knepp asked as she sat quilting with Ester. The two were close to the fire in the Phillips' farmhouse. Colin had come in several times looking around the room, smiling, and then leaving. It was clear that he was looking for someone or something.

Ester smiled at her friend. "He has been funny all morning, but it is Uri who worries me the most." Ester laid down her quilt and stretched her fingers. "Would you like coffee and cake, we seem to have been working for hours and my fingers are starting to cramp?"

"I would," Betsy said. "Let me help you."

The two women made their way to the kitchen. While Betsy filled the kettle, Ester poked the fire in the stove. Then, with a piece of cake each, they sat at the table. The farmhouse was big and comfy and so cozy with the snow falling outside the windows. "Oh, I like this," Betsy said as she picked up a carved recipe box. Flicking open the lid she scanned through the cards.

"Don't you have one?" Ester asked.

"I did," she chuckled. "But I dropped it and it smashed. Unfortunately, it was too broken to repair. I keep meaning to look for a replacement, but I have seen nothing that I like."

"We must go into the market sometime, I'm sure we could find something."

"*Jah*, are you okay? You seem worried."

"Uri has been a little distracted since the wedding, do you think he is unhappy about Leah and Abraham?" Ester asked.

"*Nee*, I don't." Betsy smiled.

"You are probably right. I know there have been a lot of changes in the house, but he welcomed me so warmly that I cannot imagine this is the problem. Perhaps, he wishes for a *fraa* of his own?"

"I did see him talking to Dinah, do you think he might have feelings for her?"

Ester nodded. "Oh, dear, if he does, we might have to help him out. Whenever he likes a girl, he is so shy he can't speak to her. Maybe you could talk to him and get him used to talking to a woman."

Betsy let out a peal of laughter. "I will do my best, but we don't have a lot in common, and if Dinah sees it..."

"Oh, I'm so pleased I'm married," Ester said with a chuckle. "Courtship is far too complicated."

Betsy smiled but it was clear that she was sad. Remembering her own marriage, no doubt, and wondering what the future held. Ester looked at her friend; at 30, Betsy was young for a widow and she wanted to broach the subject of Christmas. The last thing she wanted was for Betsy to be alone at this time of celebration. So far, she hadn't plucked up the courage which was silly. Betsy would not be insulted, they were friends. "What are you doing for Christmas?" Ester burst out.

"I haven't thought about it yet," Betsy said but she bit her lower lip before lowering her head and looking at the cake.

"You are very welcome to join us."

Betsy took a sip of her coffee. "I don't know. You have had so many changes this year, you don't want me here as well."

"I insist," Ester said. "We would all love to see you."

"*Denke.*" Betsy was quiet, subdued.

"I'm so sorry," Ester said. "You must miss him so much. I cannot imagine how awful this was for you and how hard it must be going forward."

Betsy looked up, there was moisture in her eyes. "It is, but with friends like you, it makes it so much easier."

"Maybe, you will find love again, one day," Ester said and then wished she hadn't. It was silly, but since her love and marriage, she wanted everyone to feel the same. Now, her cheeks were glowing and she wished that she had been more considerate. Just at that moment, the *boppli* kicked and she let out a grunt.

"It's not that bad," Betsy said, "or was that the *boppli* kicking?"

The two friends chuckled; they knew each other well enough to understand. "This one certainly knows how to kick. I shall be glad when he or she is here."

"I bet, and back to your question. I hope to find love again, one day, but I don't know when or where."

At that moment, Moses came into the kitchen. "*Gut* day ladies. I'm making coffee, would you like any?"

Ester noticed that there was a pink tinge to his cheeks as he looked at Betsy. Was it the cold of the day, or was he blushing?

"*Denke*, I would love a top-up," Betsy said and Ester could swear that her cheeks were a little flushed too.

"Not for me, how are things going?" Ester asked.

Moses let out a sigh. "We are nearly done; it is cold but it has been a *gut* year. We have plenty of produce to keep us going. Of course, with you ladies selling quilts, this will be our best year for as long as I can remember. We have a lot to thank you for." With this, he offered a mock bow, first to Ester and then to Betsy. "*Gut* day, ladies." With that, he picked up a tray of coffee and left the kitchen.

"Hmm," Ester said.

"What?!" Betsy asked.

"You seem a little partial to Moses."

Betsy laughed. "I do not think that would be a *gut* match. Moses is so much younger than me and no doubt wants a younger woman as a potential bride."

"You didn't deny it," Ester said. "Don't run yourself down, you look young and Moses has a sensible head on his shoulders. Besides, the heart will do as the heart wants, so don't push opportunities away that might come your way."

"I don't know, come, we should get back to work. There are many orders we have for quilts for Christmas and at this rate, it will be next Christmas before we finish them." Betsy stood.

"*Ack*, I think we will get them all done, Leah will be back soon and we work well inside in the warm house." Ester followed her and as they sat down around the fire she had a thought. "Why don't you do a special quilt, one of all different shades of green for Moses. He needs a new one, I was going to do it but... well, if you did it, I'm sure he would appreciate it, and he is very partial to green."

Betsy chuckled. "I don't know. We have so much to do."

CHAPTER FIVE

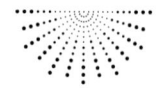

"I don't know about this," Moses Phillips said as he spoke to Colin.

Uri and Jeremiah were working in the seed store and had already finished their drinks and were back to work.

"It will work," Colin said. "You have seen how down our brother is, this is a way to make things *gut* for him, really, we would be selfish not to try.

"I think we should just tell him to talk to her. This sort of interference always goes awry." Moses was shaking his head; he had decided it was not a *gut* idea and that he would refuse.

"Please, do this, for me," Colin asked. "Uri is so shy that he just needs a little helping hand."

"Then, I should talk to her and tell her why I'm doing this. We are playing with people's lives."

Colin shook his head. "It is not like that; we are just nudging them in the right direction. You will see and you will thank me once this works. After all, no one wants to sit across the breakfast table with Uri in this mood. His face is enough to curdle the milk."

Moses laughed. "You are right there. All right, I will do it, but on your head be it, if it goes wrong."

"*Denke*, this will work, I know it will."

Moses nodded. "I was due to go to the store, so I will call on my way back." He gave his brother a stern look but Colin was smiling so brightly that he doubted he would notice.

Moses knew that Colin only meant well, but he was unsure about this idea. It seemed too complicated, but there again, what did he know about women?

It was an hour later when he arrived at the small cottage where Dinah and Conrad lived. Moses had never really taken much notice of the place, like so many, it just was. Now he looked, he realized that it was very small. Until recently, Leah had lived there too. Knocking on the door, he whispered a prayer of thanks. He had to remember all there was to be grateful for and yet, he had never seen Dinah without a smile on her face.

"Moses is it?" Dinah asked.

"*Jah*, I am the brother of Abraham who married Leah... I wondered if I could ask you something?" Moses could feel that his face was burning and his tongue seemed like an old leather slipper in his mouth. All out of control and sagging. Was this what Uri felt like? It was not because he was interested in Dinah, she was lovely, but he felt a pull in a different direction. Would he ever do anything about that? It was because he was nervous about making things worse. What if Colin was wrong?

"Do come in, my *daed* will be grateful for a visit." Dinah stepped aside.

Moses was about to say that he was not here for a visit, but it seemed so selfish. "Of course, I can only stay a few moments."

"*Daed*, we have a visitor," Dinah said. "Let me bring some refreshments, my *daed* is in here." She pushed open a door into a small living room and Moses stumbled in.

"*Ack*, Moses is it?" Conrad said. "Come and sit, the fire is warm and welcoming."

"It is, *denke*. How are you?" Moses took a seat and noted that the chairs were worn and sagging. Conrad was sitting in a wheelchair next to the fire with his Bible on his lap and a worn blanket over his knees.

"What can we do for you?" Conrad asked.

Moses felt his eyes open a little wider and his mouth dropped open. If he did what he was here for, it would give Conrad the wrong impression. What had he done?

"Do not worry, I know you are not here for me, that is fine," Conrad said. "Still, perhaps we can talk for a moment or two. You would make an old man very happy."

Moses smiled. "I would like that. Leah has married my brother, Abraham, and my brothers and I, Uri especially, wondered if Dinah was missing her. Though she is away at the moment, visiting around the district as is customary, we wondered if Dinah, and you if you are up for it, would like to join the family for dinner.

"She would love to," Conrad said as Dinah came into the room.

"I don't know. I should not leave you," Dinah said as she placed a tray with coffee and cake on a small table next to them.

"*Nee*, this is wonderful, you should go. If I am up to it, I will come too," Conrad said, "And look at this fine chocolate cake, she will make a *gut fraa*, my Dinah."

"*Daed!*" Dinah said.

Moses hoped that she had heard the full conversation, including the part about Uri. "Would you like one of us to fetch you in a buggy?" he asked, hoping she said *jah*, so he could send Uri.

"*Nee*, it is not far, the walk will be lovely in the snow."

"It is a magical time of year," Moses said. "My brother, Uri, loves the snow, sledding, throwing snowballs, just walking in it. I prefer to be next to a warm fire."

"Oh, I wish I could go out on a buggy ride in the snow again," Conrad said. "There is something about being warm and toasty beneath a blanket and yet, the chill of the air on your face."

"I'm not sure that you're well enough," Dinah said.

Moses chatted with them for a short while before making his leave. Dinah had seemed so happy, he just hoped that he had not given her the wrong impression. Oh, this was complicated.

* * *

"How did it go?" Colin asked Moses as he arrived back at the farm.

"It's all organized but I feel as if this could be a disaster."

Colin shook his head. "Don't be silly, this is perfect. Our plan to bring Dinah and Uri together is one step closer. Why do you look so worried?"

"They are not living in the best of circumstances and I don't know what to do about it."

"How do you mean?" Colin asked.

"The house is warm and clean but the furniture is... old... saggy in places and I think Dinah's dress is nearly worn through."

"I had heard Leah mentioning the same to Abraham before the wedding. They planned to help, but didn't know how." Colin shrugged his shoulders.

"That is easy, someone will be getting new furniture for Christmas, we get them to donate their old ones." Moses was shaking his head as if Colin was stupid.

"*Ack, nee*, the problem is that they are proud and wouldn't want charity. Leah said that they were happy and had everything they needed, she hadn't really noticed how poor things were until she moved away."

"That is often the way. We must get Uri to speak to Amos about it," Moses said.

"*Jah*, the bishop will know what to do." Colin felt a tinge of guilt. He was still nervous around the bishop, even though Amos had been nothing but welcoming. How would he feel about this plan of theirs? Would he help Dinah out, was he already doing so? Colin still felt as if he was an outsider, at times.

CHAPTER SIX

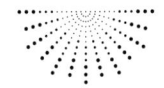

Leah looked around her new kitchen and she couldn't stop the feeling of joy. It felt like she was about to explode with happiness. They had spent a few days staying with family and would soon be back to the small house that was tucked away on the Phillips brothers' land.

The house had been empty for some years, and little be known to the couple, the brothers had arranged for it to be cleaned and readied for their arrival. It had been repaired, where needed, and given a new coat of pain. Furniture was bought and moved in and it was perfect.

The sound of the door opening made Leah's heart leap. "Abraham, is that you?"

"*Ack*, of course, it is. Where is my beautiful *fraa*?"

He walked into the room and Leah felt her heart melt. Already he was developing a beard, though you could hardly call it that, just yet. It gave her a sense of belonging to see the symbol of his marriage sprouting on his chin.

Abraham came across and bent to kiss her, the sweet taste of his lips was another joy she could not get enough of.

"I have missed you," she said as he moved away. "How long has it been?"

The icy blue eyes always looked warm to her, never cold as some had said. Now they seemed to see through to her soul as he scratched his chin in inquiry. "Only a few hours, but still, it was too long."

She chuckled and walked into his arms, kissing him once more and enjoying the feel of his sprouting beard. "How was your day?" she asked as they pulled apart.

"It was *gut*, cold, but the farm is doing so well."

"I am so pleased. I must get back to quilting as soon as we are properly home." They had two more nights to spend with relatives before they were officially home.

He put his arms around her and she leaned against his chest. "There is no need to rush back," he said. "I keep thinking about our wedding day, it was the most perfect of days. I know that our marriage is only going to get better. We have so much to look forward to... so you do not need to rush."

"We do, but you didn't make it easy. Remember, you ran away. I feared that I had lost you and if you hadn't come back, we would never have gotten to enjoy such sweet moments. What would I have done if you had left for *gut*?"

"I'm sorry for that, I never meant to hurt you. Leaving you was the loneliest of moments in my entire life, but I am not lonely now. I'm so sorry for it... sometimes life gets complicated and we men, well, we don't always know what to do, for the best."

Leah chuckled. "I certainly believe that."

"Cheeky," he said and kissed her again. "I will never get enough of your company or your kisses."

Leah stood back and smiled at him. "Or I yours. Now, let me get your dinner, it is cooking and almost ready."

Leah crossed to the range and pulled a casserole dish out of the oven. It was bubbling and the smell was delicious.

It was a lamb and dumpling stew, hearty and warming for such a cold winter's night.

"What are these?" Abraham asked.

Leah turned to see him looking at a box of decorations that she had started to make. "I wanted to cheer the place up for Christmas."

"Don't you like our home?" Abraham's face had crumpled in worry.

"*Nee*, it is not that. I just want this to be the best Christmas. I want us to enjoy it so much and I love to make a home festive."

"*Ack*, I'm jumping to conclusions again, what is wrong with me?"

"You are a man!" Leah chuckled at the look of mock horror on his face. "You know I'm only teasing. Now, wash your hands and sit at the table."

"*Jah*, ma'am." He raised his eyebrows at her before walking to the sink to wash his hands.

Leah loved watching him and once his hands were clean he splashed water over his face and beard, rubbing them to remove any dust. How she loved marriage life, and how she couldn't wait to spend her first Christmas as his *fraa*, and as part of the Phillips family. That was when it hit her, she wanted to make it special for all of them.

"What is it?" he asked.

Leah realized that she was standing there with her mouth open and his plate in her hand. She had frozen halfway between the counter and the table. "I just had an idea."

"It looked like it was hard work." He waggled his eyebrows again.

"Very funny. I want to host a Christmas dinner for all the family," she said.

Abraham smiled and then looked around the small kitchen. They also had a dining room but the house was not big, it would be a squeeze with all his brothers and their *fraas*. "I like the idea, but we are a little short on space."

"How about if I do it at the main house? I could ask Ester if she'd mind letting me host the lunch there... if I do all the work?"

"I'm sure she would be delighted. It must be quite a shock for her to go from living with Rhonda, who ate no more than a sparrow, to cooking for my brothers and me, who each eat more than a horse. *Jah,* I think that is a great idea. But you do realize that she will help and I imagine that Betsy will want to help too."

"Oh, I like the sound of that. Do you think Betsy will come for the day?"

"I think so, I just assumed she would." Abraham shrugged, only a man could make something so complicated, so simple.

Leah hoped she would, but she understood that being alone at Christmas might be what the widow needed. However, she hoped not, for she knew that Moses would enjoy having her there for the festive season.

As they ate and chatted about the day she thought of what would need to be prepared and her mind turned to wanting everyone to feel the joy she felt. Maybe it was a Christmas for matchmaking?

CHAPTER SEVEN

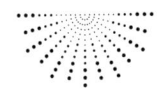

"Have a great evening," Conrad said as Dinah kissed his cheek and tucked a blanket around his knees.

"I will, are you sure you will be all right?"

"Of course, I will be. The fire is made up, I have a coffee here and cookies you have made for me. I am warm and I have my Bible, what more could I ask for?"

Dinah let mock disappointment cross her face. "I thought I'd at least be missed." She chuckled.

"Always, my little button, but I want you to live your life too. This Moses is a nice young man from a *gut* family, this is all I ever wanted for you. Go, enjoy, I will be fine."

"Your medicine is just at your side," she said.

"I can manage, go, enjoy."

Dinah kissed his cheek once more and left before her nerve failed her. Was this just a dinner invitation from the family? She was not sure if Leah was back, but if she was, it would be lovely to see her… but was this more? Her *daed* obviously thought that Moses was wanting to court her, that this was, for all intents and purposes, a date.

Dinah pulled her coat tighter around her neck and walked down the path. The snow had started to freeze and was crispy beneath her boots. She loved winter but hated wearing shoes. There was something about having your feet in contact with the earth that always felt so real. Still, in this weather, she was glad of the boots.

It was snowing gently, big fluffy flakes that seemed to float down out of a black sky. It was a lovely night for a walk and she regretted saying she would walk there alone. It was romantic… it would have been so nice to walk there with a man, almost but not quite touching hands. It was something she had often dreamed of; was this her chance?

Leah sighed as she stepped into some snow that was a little deep. She had been thinking too much and had stepped off the road and into a rut. The snow had come over her boots and was melting on her woolen tights. That would teach her to daydream.

Finding her way back to the road, she felt all wrong. It was not Moses that she felt attracted to but the red-headed Uri. As she thought about him, she could see his smiling face, and it brought a smile to her lips. Then she laughed. For someone who never expected to court, here she was upset because the wrong brother might be wanting to court her.

She stepped off the road and onto the Phillips' driveway, even though it was long and wide it had been cleared of most of the snow. The brothers were still selling their produce and wanted to keep it clear for their customers. Dinah took a deep breath, whatever would be, would be.

As she got closer to the house she could see that Moses was waiting outside, was he waiting for her?

Moses smiled as she got closer. "I hope the walk was not too bad."

"*Nee*, it was fine, glorious in fact, look at all this beauty."

Moses smiled. "I prefer a warm fire, but it is pretty." He looked down and Dinah couldn't help but notice how nervous he seemed.

"I want to say *denke* for inviting me," she said.

Moses looked up too quickly. "I... err... I need to make a confession." He stopped talking and seemed to be asking permission.

Dinah felt her heart tumble. Had she got this all wrong, maybe they didn't want her there after all. She hated to go home so soon for she knew how disappointed her *daed* would be. Not at her, but for her. "Is there a problem?" she managed to ask.

"*Nee, nee* problem... It's just... how do I put this?" His blue eyes seemed to be asking her for help.

"Whatever it is, just tell me," she said, but her heart was beating against her chest like a bird caught in a window.

"It is just that... I want to help you get to know my brother better... Uri."

Dinah felt like she had been struck. This was not what she expected. So, she was not here as a family friend and no one wanted to court her, but Moses wanted her to get to know Uri. It made no sense whatsoever.

"I did not mean to insult you," Moses said.

"You have not, I am just confused. If Uri wants to get to know me why didn't he come to see me?"

Moses shook his head. "*Ack*, he is too shy. He wants to, but would never pluck up the courage, and when he does come and talk to you, he is like an addle-headed dullard."

Dinah felt her mouth drop open and she let out a burst of laughter. She was not meaning to be cruel but the words were so unexpected. Also, now that Moses had said that, it made a lot of sense. Uri had always seemed so… confused… well, that was the kindest word she could use when he spoke to her. "I don't know what to say," she said.

"You could tell me if you like him," Moses said.

"I do." The words came out of their own volition and Dinah was shocked to hear herself say them so readily.

Moses leaned in a little closer to her. "Then maybe, if we put our heads together, we can make this a great Christmas for you and Uri. We can give my brother the best Christmas present ever."

Dinah was excited by the idea but she sucked her teeth and shook her head. "I don't know. It just feels as if this could all go wrong."

"*Nee*, it won't. We will be careful; we will stick to the idea that you are just here as a friend of the family. I could even see if I can get Uri to walk you home."

Dinah agreed. It seemed like a *gut* idea, well, maybe her only hope of courting, and Christmas was such a romantic time that she was prepared to give this a try.

"*Gut,* then let's go inside."

* * *

Betsy stood in the shadow of the tree watching Moses and Dinah speak. They were leaning in close and obviously together. Though part of her still grieved her husband, and part of her knew he was too young for her, another part was hurt and jealous. It looked like this would be a sad and lonely Christmas. It looked like Ester and her were wrong, that Moses did not like her but had his eye on another.

Betsy wiped at her eyes; were these tears or simply from the cold? Should she go home? Would it be awful to sit around the table of her friend, trying to be happy when her heart was feeling a little crushed?

It didn't matter, she had said she would come. If she didn't turn up they would worry and come looking for her. She would get through this; she had gotten through worse. As she stepped out of the trees she whispered a prayer. "*Denke, Gott,* for teaching me humility, now please just help heal my heart and let me find peace this Christmas."

Wiping her eyes and straightening her back she put a smile on her face and walked up to the house. She would get through this.

CHAPTER EIGHT

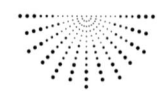

*J*eremiah turned the corner to see Colin coming out of his room. Though his brother was settling in nicely, he couldn't help a feeling of worry crawl into his stomach. Would Colin let them down once more?

Colin smiled, it was a secretive smile, a smug smile. It made Jeremiah angry for it said that he was hiding something. Jeremiah felt his body tense. He would be so angry if Colin broke their hearts once more. If he left for pastures new. If he decided that the grass on the *Englischer* side of the fence was greener than that on the Amish side, after all.

"Why are you so grumpy?" Colin asked with a smirk.

"I'm not. I was just wondering what you're up to. You caused a lot of pain by leaving and I don't want to see more of it." Jeremiah watched his brother sharply and what he saw was disappointment. Was that because he had caught him out, or because Colin was disappointed that he wasn't supporting him? Oh, how he wished their *daed* was still here, he made these things seem so easy.

"I've apologized time and time again. My life was complicated. I didn't mean to hurt you all. It was just… just that once I had stayed away so long, I didn't feel as if I could come home. I'm sorry, what more can I do?" Colin asked.

"Prove your loyalty to the family. Make life better for us as we do for you." Jeremiah was trying to moderate his tone, to sound supportive, but he could see it wasn't working. His words came out harsher than he had hoped and he saw a look of hurt cross Colin's green eyes. Swallowing, Jeremiah thought of what to say to soften the blow but Colin beat him to it.

"I am doing just that." Colin's smile was assured, even a little arrogant. "I am already trying to make things better for Uri, you will see. I can be *gut* for this family. Now, cheer up, brother, it will soon be Christmas." Colin gave a less-than-secure smile and walked away.

Jerimiah sighed. How he hoped Colin was telling the truth, that this was right. He knew that his brothers had welcomed Colin back with joy in their hearts and had forgiven everything he had done. He, however, could not quite forget the past. It was he who had to listen to their *daed's* heartbreak at never having reconciled with his son. It was he who listened to Henry's worries that it was his fault that Colin had left. Though he hoped that Colin was back for *gut*, part of him was still torn. A leopard never changed its spots, had Colin? The wayward brother had caused a lot of heartache when he left. How could they be sure that he was back for *gut*?

Jeremiah sighed, was this the reason for his reticence? A part of him wondered if he resented his brother's carefree years. Colin had left, had walked away free and easy, leaving him to be the adult. The one who had to care for them all, the one who had worked hour after hour taking it all on his shoulders. Was he resentful, maybe even a little jealous?

"What are you hiding in the corridor for?" Ester asked as she put her arms around Jeremiah and snuggled against his shoulder. "Come, husband, we have guests."

Jeremiah pulled back and kissed her lips. He gave thanks for his blessings. With this wonderful woman in his arms, he could face anything. He would have faith and trust in *Gott*; maybe, he could even trust in Colin. "Lead on, my love."

As they made their way to the dining room he knew that he had to give his brother a chance, and yet, he just kept hoping that Colin's actions would speak louder than his words.

* * *

The meal had been a chicken roast with all the vegetables and they were just about to start a shoofly pie. Ester looked around the room. Things had changed so much for her. At one time, she had just two people in her life, now, she loved all of the people here and more, and she wished she could ease all their worries.

It was clear that there was tension, but she didn't know why. Before she served the dessert she closed her eyes and prayed that *Gott* would help them all have the best Christmas that they could. That He would ease their burden and point them in the right direction.

* * *

Uri was struggling to eat and had only picked at his food. All the time, he found his eyes crossing the table, where Moses was sitting next to Dinah. It was not something he wanted to see.

Dinah was laughing and joking with his brother, her cheeks often flushed. *Were they courting?* Uri felt a flush of anger. What was his brother doing? He had only just admitted his feeling for her, and now it was too late. Would he have to spend the rest of his life seeing the woman he loved… did he love her? … with his brother?

Confusion turned his stomach and made the food seem heavy and greasy. To make matters worse, Colin and Moses seemed to be throwing Dinah in his face. They both tried to make him talk to her, and she looked so devastated at that. It made him realize that she did not care for him one bit. Perhaps she didn't even like him? The look of horror on her face when he started stuttering and babbling, like a fool, was crushing.

"Uri, tell Dinah how you love to walk in the snow," Moses said.

Uri raised his head and his throat felt so dry. Dinah was looking at him, her eyes fully on him. "I… I… I like snow. It is cold and refreshing. It… it." He shook his head and looked away as anger pinked his cheeks.

"My brother is a poet," Moses said with a laugh and he smirked at Uri.. or was he giving him an encouraging look. It was hard to tell.

What Uri had wanted to say, was that snow took his breath away. The magnificence of it painting the landscape in the glowing glory of *Gott*. That it made him feel both small and insignificant, and yet also loved, and that it filled him with the hope of the spring to come. He wanted to tell her how exhilarating it was to sled down the hill. The wind in his face, the cold in his lungs, and the joy of speed in his heart. That he would love to take her sledding or on a sleigh ride with a picnic, he would take a blanket for her knees, the stars would be above them, and he would bring a thermos of hot chocolate to enjoy. Instead, he stuttered and said it was cold. What would she think of him?

* * *

Ester looked over at her friend. Betsy was quiet, she looked so shy, so small. Was being in the family reminding her of her lost husband? Or was it something more? Sitting next to Dinah, across the table from Betsy, Moses was also acting strange. At times he was over-animated. Trying to encourage Uri to speak to Dinah, but then he looked across at Betsy, and worry lined his brow.

What had she done wrong? Ester had wanted this dinner to be the start of the preparations for Christmas. She wanted it to bring all the family together and yet there had been quarrels, petty bickering, and this strange atmosphere that hung over the room. She understood why her husband, Jeremiah, was on edge. He took everything on his shoulders. At the moment, his biggest fear was that Colin would leave and that it would break his brothers' hearts. Was he right to fear? Was that why there was an atmosphere or was something going on that she didn't know about? How she wished she understood people better. Years of living in solitude had left her with few instincts when it came to people.

*** * ***

Betsy felt her heart break into tiny pieces. She had been a fool to imagine that she could ever find love again. To think that something as perfect as a marriage with Moses was possible, was naive. He was too young for her; he was the brother-in-law of her best friend. Life was rarely this perfect. And yet, it could be! It had been in the past and wasn't that *Gott's* promise. That with faith, all things were possible?

"Who would like some Shoofly Pie?" Ester asked. The smile on her face was strained. *What was wrong with her?* Betsy wondered.

Mumbles of *Jah* went around the table and Betsy followed Ester to the kitchen to fetch the pie.

"Are you all right?" Betsy asked.

Ester put a smile on her face. "I worry about you all." She started to cut the pie and serve up the portions.

"You don't need to," Betsy said. "This has been a wonderful dinner and I am so grateful to you."

"Will you spend Christmas with us?" Ester asked, but the strain on Betsy's face was clear.

"I don't think so," Betsy said. "Maybe it is best that your family spends time together." As she said the words she had a vision of Moses staring into Dinah's eyes as they opened presents or shared a Christmas meal. It was too much for her to stand.

"I know there is an atmosphere tonight," Ester said. "I don't know why, but I know the brothers are acting strange. Maybe it is me... I don't know, but I promise it would not be like this by Christmas. Please come... or at least think about it?"

Betsy managed a smile. "I will think about it, but do not think it is you if I say *nee*."

As they served the pie, Betsy wondered if she could do this for her friend or if it would be too much like torture? Of course, her only other option was a Christmas alone! Would that be worse of better?

CHAPTER NINE

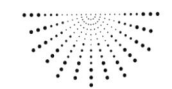

The meal was over and Betsy helped Ester clear away the table. Once they had finished she stayed in the kitchen.

"What is it?" Ester asked.

"I apologize that I was not the best of company tonight," Betsy said. "I have a headache, and I think it was a lot for me this evening. But, *denke* for inviting me."

Ester pulled her into her arms. "You are always welcome. Let me get Moses to drive you home."

"*Nee*, there is no point in taking a horse and buggy in this horrid weather. The walk is not far and I will enjoy it. I can clear my head, think and talk to *Gott* all in one go. Wish everyone a *gut* night for me."

"Are you sure?" Ester asked. "I hate to send you out there alone."

"I would never be alone with friends like you. I am sure." Betsy nodded, but she was curious, had her friend not seen what had happened tonight. Did she not realize that Moses had no interest in her? That his eyes were on another, a younger woman!

"I will try one more time, Moses would walk you home."

"*Nee*, I am sure. *Denke*." Betsy kissed Ester's cheek and grabbed her coat before stepping out into the cold. She managed a smile before the door was closed behind her. It felt like it was shutting out her future. Now, she was all alone and left in the cold. It was silly, but she felt tears on her cheeks.

"Dear *Gott*," she whispered. "Give me the strength to be a better person. To be grateful for the friends I have and the strength to wish Dinah and Moses the happiest of times. Amen."

The journey was a cold and lonely walk and she arrived back at her small and empty house. Where was her life going? What was she to do?

* * *

Ester served coffee but the talk around the table had almost stopped.

"Where is Betsy?" Moses asked.

"She went home, she was not feeling well," Ester said, though she wondered if that was the truth. Betsy had seemed so unlike her normal self.

Moses jumped to his feet. "I should see her home safely."

"*Nee*," Ester said. "I think she wanted to be by herself. Perhaps tonight brought back memories of her husband. Perhaps she needs time to be alone."

"Ah, oh, I didn't think of that." Moses sat back down looking a little lost.

Uri was staring at Moses as if he was a two-headed monster and Dinah looked miserable. With Leah and Abraham not here, that left Jeremiah still looking angry and Colin looked like the cat that had gotten the cream. What was going on? Ester wished she understood people more, for she felt that they needed her help. However, if she couldn't understand what was wrong, how could she help?

"I have had a lovely evening," Dinah said, "but I think I should go home now. *Denke* so much."

"You are very welcome," Ester said. "We enjoyed your company and you are welcome, as is your *daed*, anytime."

"That is so kind." Dinah stood and Uri was on his feet.

"Perhaps Uri can drive or walk you home?" Moses said.

Uri looked at his brother with such a look that Moses's smile dropped from his face.

"I think that you should do it," Uri said and then he pushed back his chair and left the room without another word.

"What is going on?" Jeremiah asked and he turned to Dinah. "I apologize, my brother is not normally this rude. I do not know what is wrong with him."

The smile had slipped off Colin's face and Moses's mouth was opening and closing a little like a goldfish.

"It is all right," Dinah said. "*Denke* once more and I wish you all a *gut* night."

She walked to grab her coat and boots but Moses was there with her. "I will walk you home."

"*Denke*, but that is not necessary. I know you tried... but it is not to be." She smiled and put on her boots. The left one was wet and cold from where she had stepped off the path. The cold was a wake-up call. She had dared to dream but that dream was foolish.

"I insist," Moses said and he turned to look at Colin, giving his brother a desperate look. It said, *what have we done?*

Once they were outside, Dinah let out a big breath. She felt like she had been on edge all evening. All the time she was pretending to be happy when she now knew that Uri wanted nothing to do with her. The look he had given her was enough to freeze her heart and he had not wanted to speak to her, no matter how much his brothers tried. It had been painful.

"I know that this was a disaster," Moses said.

"It does not matter, you tried and I appreciate it. Uri is not the man I thought he was," Dinah said.

"Oh, are you no longer interested in him? Did his... rambling put you off him? If it did, I can assure you that he is only like that around you."

Dinah bit back the lump in her throat. That said it all. He was different around her, maybe he disliked her so much that he hated to see her there.

CHAPTER TEN

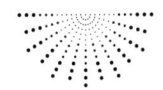

"*Nee, nee*, you are thinking the wrong thing," Moses said. "I can see it all over your face."

"I understand," Dinah said. "There is no need to try to make me feel better."

"Oh, but there is. I think our plan backfired. I think that he thought that I was with you. I brought you there for him... but it all went so wrong."

"I do not know."

"Trust me, I will talk to him and I will make this right."

They had arrived at Dinah's home and she could see that the curtains were drawn. Her *daed* must have wheeled himself over so that he could watch for her coming home. It also meant that he had now seen Moses walking her. Oh, dear, this was getting worse and worse.

"I think you'd better say *gut* night to my *daed*!" Dinah shrugged her shoulders. "I will tell him we are just friends."

A look of worry crossed Moses's face for a moment, and then he smiled.

They walked into the living room, where Conrad had a big smile on his face. "*Gut* evening, young Moses. Did you both have a lovely time?"

"*Jah*, we did, *Daed*, but Moses is just a friend."

"*Ack*, I understand," Conrad said and patted his nose.

Dinah knew that he wouldn't believe her and that she had this to face in the future, but for now, she was tired.

"Would you make some coffee?" Conrad asked her. "Here, Moses, come and sit with me. It is always nice to talk."

Dinah gave Moses an apologetic smile but he returned a genuine one and sat down with her *daed*. They were talking instantly and she left them to make the coffee.

Once in the kitchen, she made some cocoa instead of coffee. While she waited for the kettle, she could hear voices in the other room. Though she could not hear what was said, she knew that her *daed* was enjoying the conversation. Moses appeared to be too. Maybe tonight hadn't been such a total disaster. Anything that gave her *daed* comfort was worth any price.

"*Ack*, it blew the barn door off. Abraham was standing there with it in his hands. It looked as if it would knock him over. The look on his face." Moses chuckled.

"I would love to have seen that, what did you do?" Conrad asked as Ester handed him a cocoa.

Moses chuckled even more. "We were finding it so funny that we were frozen to the spot. Abraham was wavering, the door was heavy. It was only at the last moment, that we ran around and helped him put it down. I think if we had taken much longer he would have sailed away on the wind with it. It was not so funny later as we had to spend a *gut* few hours putting it back on, in a high and bitter wind. Still, with us all working together we got it done."

"That is what family are for," Conrad said. "Don't you agree, Dinah? Being part of a big family is a blessing."

"That is true, *Daed,* maybe Moses should be on his way. It is late and cold out."

"*Ack,* I guess so. I have enjoyed your company." Conrad looked at Moses and then pointedly looked at Dinah. "You are welcome here any time."

"*Denke,* and *gut* night."

Dinah showed Moses to the door. "I'm sorry that he thinks we are courting."

"It is *nee* problem. He is a joy to talk to. Do not worry. I will help put things right."

Dinah thanked him once more and watched him walk out into the gently falling snow. She wished he could, but in her heart, she knew there was no chance.

* * *

Jeremiah heard Ester say Amen and climb into bed. As always, they had no light on while they prayed. They could see a little by the light of the moon. With the snow outside, it made the room lighter than normal, and tonight he felt strange. Something was wrong with his brothers but he didn't know what.

Normally, his prayers were easy and relaxing, a way of expressing his worries and his gratitude. Tonight, he had no idea what to say. It was disturbing.

"Come to bed," Ester said. "You are thinking too much. *Gott* will be happier if you sleep on it."

"*Ack*, you are probably right," he said. "Amen."

He climbed into bed and pulled her into his arms. She was toasty against the chill of the room and the bed was already warming. He reached around and touched her tummy and she snuggled deeper into his arms.

"This is my favorite time of the day," he said.

"Mine too, oh, did you feel that?"

"I did, he is kicking. You can tell it's a boy, that was one strong kick."

Ester grunted. "Then he is not a gentleman, I will be having words with him once he gets here." She chuckled. "I can't wait to meet our *boppli*, whatever it may be."

"Me either, you have made me so happy."

Ester chuckled. "Really! Then why the long face?"

"You can't see my face; you have your back to me."

"I don't need to see it; it is ingrained in my mind from tonight."

"Oh, I'm so sorry. You know how much I worry about Colin. Tonight, I felt as if he was hiding something. As if something he was keeping from me was making him feel superior. It made me uneasy, what if he leaves again? What if he destroys Christmas?"

Ester pulled away from him and rolled over so she was facing him. She kissed his lips and took his hand and put it on her swollen stomach. "We have this *boppli* coming and nothing else matters. Families will squabble, but they will make amends. Colin is not leaving. He may have worries or even secrets, but that is nothing to worry about. Perhaps, he just got you a Christmas gift and is feeling smug. Perhaps the brothers are planning something for you. Do not let it spoil things between you."

"I know you are right, but you are also worried, why, my love?"

"Something upset Betsy tonight and I don't know what. Also, what was wrong with Uri? He was rude to Dinah and I thought he liked her?"

"Uri likes Dinah?" Jeremiah asked.

"Are you blind? Of course, he does."

Jeremiah kissed her again. "Courting is not easy, I'm so glad that it is behind us and we have only *gut* times ahead."

Ester chuckled. "Say that to me when the *boppli* is waking us up all night!"

"I can't wait."

"Neither can I, I just hope that everyone can sort things out for Christmas. Is that too much to ask?"

"*Nee*, my love, it isn't. Now, you relax and sleep. I love you," Jeremiah said as he kissed her once more.

"I love you too." As she rolled over to sleep, Ester worried about her friend. Was Betsy just tired or had something upset her?

CHAPTER ELEVEN

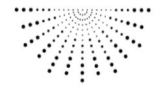

Dinah pulled the chicken out of the oven as she heard the knock on the door.

"He's here," her *daed* called. "I'll get it."

Dinah smiled and continued to work on the meal. Her *daed* seemed so well at the moment. He was getting around the house in his wheelchair and being so much happier. Dinah knew it was because he thought she was courting Moses. At first, she had told him they were just friends but he wouldn't listen. Today, she hadn't had the heart to tell him otherwise. Of course, this dinner with Moses would only make it seem more like they were courting. What was she to do?

"*Gut* day, Dinah," Moses said as he took off his hat and coat.

"*Gut* day, there is a coat hook on the door." Dinah pointed with her head as she carried the dish to the table. Potatoes were already there in tureens as were the vegetables. They were almost the last she had managed to grow this year. Though she knew Bishop Beiler would bring her some soon, she wondered if it would be in time for Christmas. What would she do if there was no food for Christmas day?

She shook her head; she must pray on it. They had always managed before and she would manage now. Maybe some of her customers would bring a Christmas gift. It had happened before; it could happen again. One thing she knew, was if her neighbors knew that they were struggling, then things would appear. Maybe she should let them know... but she hated to do that. She wanted to manage.

"Are you okay?" Moses asked.

Dinah nodded and took him through to the dining room.

Soon, they were eating and talking and it was all so nice. Dinah enjoyed Moses's company but she knew he had no interest in her and she couldn't help but wish it was Uri.

"These are wonderful dumplings," Moses said.

"She is an excellent cook, my Dinah," Conrad said, "she would make a man a *gut fraa*."

"*Daed*! I have told you that Moses and I are just friends. He has come to see you as much as me."

"Do not be silly." Conrad had a smile on his face. "I was young once, you know. Now, young man, tell me about your farm. What are you selling at this time of year?"

Moses smiled. It was clear that he enjoyed talking with Conrad. At least that had come out of this, but she was still no closer to finding out if Uri would like to court her or not. As the days passed, she began to think it was just a dream, and that Moses kept coming out of obligation. What should she do?

"Well, we had an excellent year and managed to can and bottle a lot of our crop," Moses said. "We are selling many of those, the strawberries and raspberries were so *gut* this year. We also have potatoes and the quilts that the ladies make. They have been such a boost to the farm, they turned it around."

"I guess this is the time of year for resting and recuperating after a hard harvest," Conrad said.

"It is, the work is hard, and the hours are long in the season but it is worth it. I love to be outside in the summer, I'm not so keen on it in this weather."

"Oh, well... unlike this one," Conrad waved his hand at Dinah and she felt her cheeks burn. "Now she loves to walk in any weather. It takes me all my time to make sure she has her shoes on. She would go out in the snow barefoot if I let her."

"*Daed*, you know that's not true."

"Not quite, but close enough." He chuckled.

Dinah was so pleased to see him so happy that she chuckled too. "Let me get the dessert. It's a lemon meringue pie."

"*Ack*, my favorite," Conrad said. "What is your favorite, Moses?"

As she dished up the pie she could hear the two men talking. It seemed that Moses liked chocolate cake, especially warm and with cream. She would make sure that she made him some if he came again.

They talked for a couple more hours until Conrad began to cough. It was almost instant. The color drained from his face and he coughed so much that he began to choke. Dinah got him his medicine and helped him take it. The coughing stopped but it was clear that he was drained. Exhausted from too much enjoyment. It was *gut* to see.

"It has been so *gut* to have you here, but I fear I must retire. Stay and chat with Dinah and come back whenever you wish, *gut* night."

Dinah pushed him to his room and helped him get ready and into bed.

"I like him, he would be *gut* for you, my sweet Dinah."

"I know, *Daed*." She kissed his cheek and shut the door. She didn't have the heart to tell him that they weren't courting, again.

"Is he all right?" Moses asked.

"*Jah*, he is, but he will not listen when I tell him we are just friends."

"I know, he was the same with me." Moses shrugged. "He just kept tapping his nose and smiling. I think, the sooner we get you and Uri together, the better."

"I don't think that will be possible." Dinah felt so sad that it was crushing. For so long she expected to remain single, now she had seen a touch of hope, and it was devastating to lose it.

Moses smiled. "Do not lose faith, there must be a way."

"How?"

"I will make it right. In the meantime, Uri loves to go birdwatching early in the morning. He is often up before the sun rises and likes to walk along the creek bed. Perhaps, there is a way that you could meet. Maybe a conversation could start from there?"

"*Jah*, that is a *gut* idea. My *daed* rarely wakes before the sun is high in the sky. I could leave him a note, just in case, and a walk would do me *gut*."

"Maybe wear shoes!" Moses chuckled.

"I will do my best."

"I must go now," Moses said. "I have had a lovely time."

Dinah walked him to the door and walked out with him. The sun was setting and it was just starting to get dark. There was a chill in the air but it had that fresh feel. The snow had stopped and the sky was black and filled with stars; beneath the light of the moon, the snow sparkled.

"It was a lovely meal and your *daed* is great," Moses said.

"*Denke* for coming."

He reached out and took her hands and squeezed them gently. "Do not worry, we will fix this."

Dinah smiled and didn't notice that across the lane, Betsy had been walking past. As she saw the two of them together, she dived behind a tree, what was she doing?

CHAPTER TWELVE

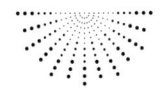

Betsy needed a walk. The house had seemed stuffy, and claustrophobic, and so she left the warmth of her rooms for the frosty chill of the night. It had been a few days since the disastrous meal at the Phillips' farm. Ester had been trying to tell her that Moses was still interested in her. That he sat next to Dinah for no reason, but she couldn't quite believe it.

After her conversation with Ester, where she said Moses would love a green quilt, she had begun work on one for him. It would make a wonderful Christmas gift, that would signal her interest.

Each night she had spent time finding the best green patches of material to make the quilt. Already she had built up a lovely store and she began to sew it the night before the meal. However, since the meal, she had not picked it up. Each evening she stared at it and it seemed to mock her. Many times, she wished to start sewing but she couldn't bring herself to do so. What was she to do?

That was why she was walking on this cold and lonely night. The moon was large in the sky and it reflected off the snow, making it almost as light as day and yet it had a surreal quality that magnified her solitude. At one time, she would have found this walk magical, but not now. What was she to do?

These words had been going through her head again and again. *What was she to do?* She hated it, for it tasted of self-pity. Betsy was not one to wallow in her own despair. However, she felt as if life was being cruel. Here she was, being helped by a friend and believing she was special to Moses and then it was taken away.

Of course, she had never spoken to Moses about her feelings. Should she?

Nee, it was too soon for that.

Walking, she prayed, asking *Gott* to give her strength and show her a sigh. Was Ester right, did Moses like her?

Or was this empty feeling inside, a confirmation that he was courting Dinah?

Looking around she realized that she was close to Dinah and Conrad's small cottage. Maybe she should call in and ask her? Well, not ask her outright, but she could hint and see if Dinah offered the information. Would that be acceptable? Of course, she could say she was passing and wondered if Dinah needed anything.

Feeling as if she had a purpose, she increased her pace just as the door to Dinah's place opened. Betsy felt her heart stop as she saw Moses coming out. Quickly, she ducked behind a tree, not caring that the snow was deeper and that both her feet and her ankles had sunk into it. Ignoring the cold, she peered around the tree.

This was awful, Moses reached forward and took Dinah's hands. He leaned in close and Betsy stopped breathing, was he to kiss her?

It didn't happen and Moses walked away with a wave of *gut* night.

Betsy stayed shadowed against the tree until he was gone and Dinah had closed the door. It was only then that she realized how cold her feet were. Biting back her tears, she made her way home. Now she knew!

* * *

Leah walked into the Phillips' farmhouse and somehow it all felt different. Now she was part of the family and it filled her with joy. It was a beautiful morning and she couldn't wait to experience the day.

Ester turned to see her and a big smile came on her face. "Come here, sister," Ester said and pulled Leah into a big hug. "How is married life?"

Leah hugged her back and then pulled away. "It is wonderful, as you very well know. It is so *gut* to be your sister, and to be here... oh, look, you are getting bigger by the day." Leah chuckled as Ester put on a sad face.

"Are you calling me fat?"

"*Nee*, it is all a strapping *boppli*, who I can't wait to meet. Aunty Leah will spoil, her/him every day."

"I know you will, come, let us have a coffee before we start." Ester put on the kettle.

"Let me do that," Leah said taking it from her. "Where is Betsy?" She was hoping to have a little time with Ester alone as she wanted to pitch her idea of doing Christmas for the family.

Ester sat down and a frown crossed her face, though she hid it quickly.

"Don't do that, not to me," Leah said and joined her at the table.

"I'm just worried about her," Ester said. "Since the dinner I did a few nights ago, she has been so quiet. I think something is wrong... or maybe she just misses her husband as we get closer to Christmas. Am I reading too much into this?"

"I don't know, we will see how she is later. If there is a problem we can help, if she just needs support, we are here for her."

"*Denke*," Ester said.

Leah made the coffee and returned to the table. "Have you thought anything about Christmas yet?"

Ester rolled her eyes. "It is worrying me. It will be the first time I have to make such a large meal and I hate to admit it, but I am pooping myself out a little with worry."

Leah burst out laughing. "That is one way to put it... I understand, it is a little scary."

"I'm also worried because of this." Ester put her hands on her belly. "I'm not quite as agile as I was."

"Then this is perfect," Leah said.

Ester gave her a strange look. "Really?"

"*Jah*, I wanted to ask if I could do the Christmas lunch here for all the family. I really want to do it... but our place is too small."

"Oh, you are a miracle," Ester said. "However, I will help.

"*Nee*. You should leave matters to me, relax and enjoy this pregnancy."

Ester chuckled. "I am already much more relaxed, but you too should be enjoying your new marriage. Trust me, I can help. However, I'm so relieved that you will take on the bulk of the work."

At that moment Moses walked into the kitchen and made himself a coffee. "Ladies," he said before walking out with his head down.

"What was that?" Leah asked.

"That was another one of my worries. Something is going on with the brothers, but I don't know what."

"Then we must get to the bottom of it," Leah said. "I just want everyone to feel the joy I feel this Christmas."

Ester chuckled. "I know what you mean, love is grand. *Ack*, here is Betsy, let's grab another coffee."

CHAPTER THIRTEEN

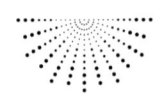

Moses was deep in thought. There had to be some way he could make his brother understand. So far, he had tried to talk to Uri, but it had not gone well. Uri was angry, dismissive, and not prepared to listen. It was clear that he was convinced that Moses had stolen Dinah and would not listen to anything that he had to say. He was hiding his hurt with indignation but it didn't fool Moses.

Then there was Colin, who was convinced that his plan was working and that true love would be in the air before Christmas. Oh, why had he agreed to do this?

"Ladies," Moses said as he walked out of the kitchen with his coffee. It only just occurred to him, that he had walked past them without an acknowledgment. Was he really that deep in thought that he would forget his manners? He must be careful, that was not the sort of man he wanted to be.

The front door opened and a cold breeze swirled around him, but it was driven away by a flush of heat. Betsy walked in and took off her boots and coat. A hat covered her *kapp*. She pulled it off grabbing her *kapp* to keep it steady, revealing just a flash of her brown hair, it was glorious, a rich walnut color. *Stop it! He should not be staring at her.* There was a flush to her cheeks from the cold and she looked beautiful, it was hard to turn away.

Moses swallowed a lump and realized that he had frozen on the spot. Here he was, worried about his brother's romance and maybe he should be concentrating on his own. Would she ever consider him?

Walking up to her, he was filled with hope. "Morning, Betsy," he said.

She raised her head and a frown crossed her features and there was a cool look in her blue eyes, eyes that previously had always seemed so warm. *What had he done?* "How was your walk?"

"It was a cold night and I got quite a shock," she said and began to walk past him.

Moses stepped in front of her. "Night?" he asked confused, "what shock?"

Betsy said nothing and began to go around him. Moses felt his heart stutter, what was wrong? They had always got on before, he felt as if they had a connection, and now... where had it gone?

"I love this time of year," he said, stepping in front of her with his biggest smile. She would hardly look up at him. "I was wondering what you like for Christmas?" He knew that this was lame and felt as if he was in a nightmare. Nothing was going to plan and he felt out of control... *nee*, things were out of his control. It was a subtle difference but one that stated clearly, that she was in control.

Betsy took a step around him and looked back. Her face was blank, devoid of any emotion. "I hope that you are happy with your choice," she said before avoiding his eyes and walking away. As she entered the kitchen she closed the door behind her and he was shut out. As he stared at the closed door he felt that he was shut out, both metaphorically and literally, what had happened?

Moses was, once more, frozen on the spot, *what had changed? What had he done? What were his choices?*

"*Gut* morning, brother," Colin said in a jolly voice as he came into the hallway. "How are you this fine morning?"

Moses shook his head. "Confused," was all he could manage.

"Then let us drink coffee and talk," Colin said and began to lead Moses to the kitchen door.

"*Nee*, I have a coffee and don't want to go in there right now."

Colin stared at him and shook his head. "Let's go to the dining room. The ladies will soon start to quilt in the living room, next to the big fire, we can talk in there and you can tell me what this is about." Colin had a big smile on his face and it made Moses feel a little better.

Sitting at the table, Moses hugged his coffee and felt a little selfish that he had not allowed Colin to get his own.

"What is it?" Colin asked.

"I have upset Betsy... I thought that we were getting close... I had even wondered about asking her if I could drive her to the next service."

Colin's mouth fell open and his eyes widened. Then a big grin came on his face, he stood up crossed the room, and slapped Moses on the back. "I am so proud of you, this is fantastic."

"*Nee*, you didn't hear me right. It was bad... something has gone wrong and now she will not look at me, will not talk to me, and told me that she hopes I'm happy with my choices. What have I done wrong?"

Colin slapped his own forehead. "I fear that I may have caused this problem, but do not fear. Women think too much and she will have gotten the wrong idea very soon. I will do right by you. I will solve this and bring you and Betsy together as I have done with Uri and Dinah."

Moses felt his own mouth drop open, Colin's plan had not worked with Uri, it had made things worse. It was then that the realization struck him. Was this also Colin's fault? Did Betsy think that he was with Dinah? This was terrible, how were they to fix it?

"Do not look so worried," Colin said. "I know about these things. I was in a relationship, remember. I understand women and I will make sure that everything is right. It is my dream to have Uri happy by Christmas; now, I will make it my dream to do the same for you."

"But... I think this is making things worse," Moses said pleading with his eyes for his brother to listen to him.

"*Nee*, trust me, I will work it out."

Moses smiled, why did his brother have to use the trust card? Now, he had to let him try, and yet, his heart said he should tell Betsy everything. Only, how did he do that? Life was too complicated, too complicated by far.

CHAPTER FOURTEEN

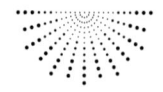

EARLY THE FOLLOWING MORNING

Uri walked out of the house with a coffee in a thermos and a blanket over his shoulder. The sun was just rising and it looked like it would be a glorious day. It painted the sky orange and red and spoke of the magnificence to come.

Uri loved this time of day. He could sneak out of the house and get some quiet time, alone, just him and *Gott's* earth waking with the dawn. Then, there were the birds, he loved to watch them, to keep a note of them in his journal. Only, this morning he had forgotten his journal, perhaps his mind was not on the birds, but on a certain young lady.

He walked automatically. The snow was frozen and crunched beneath his boots. The chill in the air was invigorating and woke him fully. Last night's sleep was still in his eyes and he felt that his legs weighed a ton. Uri was not used to staying awake all night. He usually fell asleep as soon as his head hit the pillow but recently, worrying thoughts kept him awake. Tossing and turning until the small hours of the morning as his stomach churned and his mind with it. Over and over things tumbled in his mind until he was so confused that he couldn't work out what to think. This would not do.

Before he knew it, he had walked to his normal spot. It was under the shade of a willow tree, so if he kept still, he was out of sight. The birds would come close, unable to see him beneath the branches. Today, he laid his blanket down on the bank, away from the tree. It was warmer here and he had no interest in the birds this morning. *Then why did you get out of bed?*

Uri sighed and poured a coffee from his thermos. It steamed in the cold air and warmed his fingers. Taking a sip, he reveled in the heat traveling down his gullet.

Why had he come?

The question was not an easy one to answer. Well, in part it was. He was beating himself up for falling for Dinah. Was he a fool? Did they share a connection? At one time, he had been certain of it. He was sure that she liked him and he was building up the courage to ask her to service. Often, he could see Ester looking at him with a knowing look. Did she pity him or was she on his side? Maybe, he should ask her. Ester had fitted into the family well and was an asset, not only to Jeremiah but to all the brothers. Her calming influence and wonderful cooking had changed things for the better.

Taking a sip of coffee, he sighed, should he have been more direct? What if Moses wasn't courting her, what if he had just invited her there as a friend? What if he had invited her to help Uri? None of it made sense; if that was the case, why hadn't his brother told him first?

Nee, Moses had his eye on Dinah, but what was he going to do about it?

Should he forget her and wish Moses well? Or should he fight, well, not fight, that would not be Amish, but should he lay his cards on the table, as Colin sometimes said?

Closing his eyes, he began to pray, asking for a sign and asking for the peace of mind to cope with whatever happened. "Amen," he said aloud and opened his eyes to see Dinah walking toward him.

Her cheeks were flushed and for a moment, she looked as if she would turn and run. Was that because she didn't want to see him? He guessed that was his sign.

* * *

Dinah left the house early and was finding herself delighted and excited to be out in the open. For so many years, she had done nothing for herself. That did not matter, she loved caring for her *daed,* but now, she realized that there was nothing to stop her from taking an early morning walk. It would do her *gut* and would give her a little peace and time on her own.

Suddenly, it didn't matter if she met Uri, she would continue to take a walk at least 4 times a week. Breathing in a big breath of frigid air she felt alive and free. It truly was wonderful. As she walked through the crisp snow, she thanked *Gott* for such a beautiful morning.

Without even thinking about it she followed the river bank in the direction Moses had told her. Before long, she saw Uri sitting on a blanket close to the river. His behavior surprised her; surely, he would be better beneath the branches of the willow tree? He would be out of sight and more likely to see birds. That was when she noticed that he was praying and she froze, not wanting to disturb him. Should she turn around?

Just as she had that thought, he said Amen and lifted his head. As his eyes saw her, they opened wide and there was a look of worry on his face.

What had she done? It was clear that he did not want to see her.

For a moment, she hesitated. Should she just acknowledge him and walk away? *Nee*, that would be rude. They would have to learn to get on together.

"I'm sorry to disturb you," Dinah said. "I just wanted to get out of the house." How foolish had she been to think that this would work? No man was interested in her, she had nothing to offer but a burden. How she hated to think like that for her *daed* was not a burden to her... but he did not make her a *gut* marriage prospect. Not that she ever got out to court. Oh, she should have stayed at home, she began to turn to walk away.

CHAPTER FIFTEEN

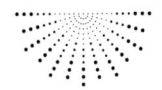

"*Nee,* you have not disturbed me," Uri said standing up. "I just came to watch the birds... I... d... d... do it some mornings... b... b..." Frustrated he dropped his eyes and shook his head turning from her.

"I'm sorry," she said, suddenly realizing that he was shy and that was why he stuttered. "I use to stutter and babble at times. The *kinner* laughed at me but my *daed* told me to ignore them and said that, if I did, I would get over it. I'm sorry if I upset you."

"*Nee,* you didn't." He shrugged. "Sometimes, I get tongue-tied and then I get angry... at myself, not at you."

"I understand," she said. "Do you come here often?" It was such a silly thing to say that she almost chuckled, but she saw something in his eyes, excitement, perhaps.

"I do, most mornings, but usually I am beneath the tree. There is an old log there that I can sit on, I like to watch the birds. It is a fabulous spot as the water birds come to the river. It is wide and slow here, perfect for them to fish and drink. Then there are the hedges," he pointed at the other side of the bank. "They are ideal for nesting for the other birds. Sorry, you don't want to hear this, it must be boring to you."

"*Nee*, it is very interesting," she said and she could see a big smile come over his face. Had she been wrong about him?

"Would you like to sit? I only have one cup but we could share my coffee." His eyes widened. "I'm sorry, you are probably disgusted at such a suggestion."

"*Nee*, it is very kind of you and a warm coffee would be most welcome." She stepped over to the blanket and sat down. Pleased when he joined her.

For a moment, he was quiet and looked away, then he poured her a coffee and handed her the cup.

"This is delicious," she said after taking a sip. "And very warming." She handed him the cup and he took a sip before passing it back.

"What is it about birds that you find so interesting?" she asked as they sat by the river drinking coffee. The blanket was lined so they were dry but it was so strange to be sitting on the ground, well, on the snow-covered ground with him as if it was normal.

Uri looked up at the sky and sighed. "You will think me foolish."

"Never," she said shaking her head and looking at him. *My, he was handsome.*

Uri took a deep breath and let it out slowly. "It is the ability to fly, the power of being able to go anywhere, above everything, and to just fly away from... well, from anything. It fascinates me.."

"I understand," she said. "What a gift to be able to take to the air and find a new home whenever you wish."

Uri turned to her, concern on his face. "Do you wish to escape your life?"

"*Nee*, that is not what I mean... though, sometimes, in my *daed's* darker moments, the thought of getting away has crossed my mind." Her hand flew to her chest and she knew her cheeks were red. "Never, for more than a moment. I love him so much and would do anything for him."

Uri was staring at her; his green eyes and red hair made him stand out from his brothers. Those eyes seemed to see right into her soul and she felt calm. It was strange, after what she had just told him, she expected to be worried, ashamed, anything but calm.

"I understand," he said. "I must compliment you on always doing right by Conrad. He is lucky to have such a loyal and caring daughter."

"Anyone would do the same," she said as her cheeks burned even more.

"*Nee*, many would care for him, but some would resent him for it. I have seen the love you have for him and have never seen even a hint of resentment from you, only love."

"*Denke*, I will always keep those that I love close and look after them whatever they need."

"I understand. I... I..." Uri stopped speaking and took a sip of the coffee. He had been about to admit his feelings and knew that it was too soon. "Oh, look," he said and pointed at the river as a pair of birds landed.

"What is it?" she asked, leaning in close so that she could whisper.

"It is a pair of Wigeon, the male is the one with the green head."

"How lovely."

"*Ack*, Jeremiah would not like too many of them here. See the blue-gray bills with the black end? They are short and powerful, good for ripping out vegetation."

"They are very pretty though, are they rare?"

"*Nee*, not really. I'm sorry if you wish to continue on your walk, I understand."

"*Nee*, it is nice sitting here. Is there any more coffee?"

He poured the rest out of the thermos and they talked about birds. He knew so much and she was fascinated, so much so that the time flew by. As the sun climbed higher in the sky she shook her head. "I have to go back; I don't want my *daed* to wake up alone."

"Of course, I will walk you."

Together they walked and occasionally she let her fingers brush against his. They were warm and he didn't move away. As she got to the gate she turned. "I hope to catch you another morning."

"I would like that." He turned to walk away.

"Uri," she called and grabbed his hand. He turned back and she held his hand in hers. It was warm, almost hot and strong, much bigger than hers. "Would you like to have dinner with my *daed* and me?"

A big smile crossed his face. "I would love to." For a moment he was going to walk away, but a feeling of joy had loosened his lips. "Would you like to spend Christmas at my house? Leah is doing a big meal for all the family; you would be very welcome."

"I would love to... if my *daed* is well enough..."

"You would both be welcome."

CHAPTER SIXTEEN

Uri almost skipped on his way back to the farm. Though in places, the snow was deep, his footsteps were light, almost childlike. It had been some time since he had felt so happy, it was almost like the joy was bubbling out of him. Though his hands were cold, and the blanket was damp, his spirits were anything but. With a big smile on his face, he walked into the kitchen and hung his blanket over a chair.

Quickly, he washed the thermos and turning around, found himself face-to-face with Colin. "What a lovely morning it is," he said.

Colin raised his eyebrows. "It is *gut* to see you in such a great mood."

Oh, dear, he felt his cheeks heating and knew that he was blushing. Quickly, he turned away from his brother and fiddled with the dishcloth, hoping he had gotten away with it.

"Not so quickly, what are you hiding?" Colin asked as he came around the table to get a better view of Uri's face.

"I met Dinah, this morning, down by the riverbank. I had this belief that she was courting Moses, but she isn't." A cloud came over his joy, dampening it, momentarily. For, he hadn't asked her if she was courting Moses. *Nee*, she would not do that. Perhaps, she had just come to the house as a friend? "But we spoke for hours and we had so much in common," he said pushing his worries away.

"That is wonderful to hear, I knew that you two had something special between you. Are you seeing her again?"

Uri felt a sense of warmth fill him, for he was. "I'm having dinner at her house tomorrow night, and, I invited her and Conrad to come over for Christmas." Uri felt a huge smile on his face and saw it reflected in his brothers. Colin was pleased for him. Until that moment, he hadn't realized how much that meant to him. It was great to have Colin back, but up until now, he had been here, but not really fitting in. That smile made him think that Colin was really on his side.

"That is wonderful, I know that Ester and Leah will be over the moon to hear that."

Uri's smile froze on his face. "I never thought to ask them first! Will this put a massive burden on them? Oh, why didn't I think this through?"

Colin slapped him on the back and shook his head. "Neither of them will mind, in fact, they will be delighted. Why don't you go tell them now? Jeremiah has said that you and I are not needed today. It is cold in the barn and there was little to do. He and Moses have got it covered."

Uri nodded, but he still had the tightness of worry in his chest. What would he do, if Ester said that they couldn't accommodate two extra guests? And now, he had all day to worry about it.

"I can see that you are worrying too much," Colin said with a chuckle. "Ester and Leah are in the living room. Why don't you go talk to them? And then, you better think of a gift to get Dinah for Christmas."

With that, Colin made himself a coffee and left the kitchen, leaving Uri standing there panicking about which way to turn. Well, he may as well face the music first, as Colin sometimes said.

Quickly, he made three coffees and cut three portions of coffee cake, and placed them on a tray. His hands were hardly shaking as he pushed the door into the living room open with a big smile. "I know how hard you ladies are working and I thought you might enjoy a break."

A big smile came over Ester's face, but Leah raised her eyebrows.

"What is he after?" Leah asked.

Ester chuckled. "It must be something pretty big if he was bribing us with cake and coffee."

Uri was standing there with the tray and suddenly he didn't know whether to stay or to turn and go. He must've done a funny little jig backward and forward because the two ladies started laughing.

"It is all right," Ester said. "We would love a break, come and join us."

Uri put the tray down and served the ladies their drink. It was both nice and annoying, for they were chuckling and sharing secret looks. It was clear that they knew he wanted to ask something. He hoped that it was also clear that they wouldn't really mind.

"Let's put him out of his misery," Ester said.

"I don't know, I think we could tease him a little more," Leah said.

"I just want to invite Dinah and Conrad for Christmas day," Uri let the words flow out of him so fast that it was almost garbled.

"What do you think?" Leah asked with her left hand on her jaw and her eyebrows pulled down.

"Well... well, it would mean two extra guests," Ester said and then started to chuckle. "Oh, I can't keep this up any longer. We had already decided we were going to ask them both to come. You did us a big favor. And if this means what I think it means, we are both delighted to have them here."

Uri let out a big sigh. "You were so much nicer when you were shy!" he said to Ester.

Ester and Leah chuckled. "You do make a good cup of coffee. Now, have you thought about what you're going to get her for Christmas?"

Uri felt his heart tumble. What did you get someone you were courting for Christmas? "Colin just said the same thing to me, and I have no idea!"

"When did you invite her?" Leah asked.

Though he tried to stop it, Uri knew that his face spread into a big smile. "I met her on the riverbank this morning. We got talking, it was so easy to talk to her, and I walked her back to her house. She invited me to have dinner with her and Conrad."

"He's got it bad," Leah said.

"He certainly has," Ester said, and turned to look at Uri. "You said she was easy to talk to, what did you talk about? Was there anything special about it? Maybe she needs new gloves?"

"Oh, how about some of those chocolates from that store in Bird-in-Hand?" Leah said. "I would love some of those."

However, something Ester had said put a thought in Uri's mind. He had an idea for the perfect gift. "*Denke*, ladies, you have been very helpful."

CHAPTER SEVENTEEN

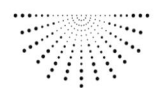

Uri wanted to make Christmas special for Dinah. He knew she had it hard, her dresses were nowhere near new, they were most definitely old and worn. At first, he had thought about buying her some material or some new dresses, but that just didn't sit right with him. She was too proud and he understood that. He would not want someone to point out what he did not have. What he would like, was something special.

Leaving the house, he made his way to the woodpile. It was well-stocked with chopped wood ready for the fire. At first, he stared at the pile. Though it was neatly stacked he had done this many times before. If he looked at it long enough, something would call to him.

A slap on the back had him jumping, almost out of his skin, and he turned to see Colin laughing at him.

"What are you staring at?" Colin asked. "If wood is needed inside, grab some logs, and let's go!"

"There is plenty inside. I'm looking for the right piece, the piece that contains..." The last thing he wanted to do was explain to Colin that if he looked at wood long enough, one piece would show him what he needed. He was looking for a piece of wood that contained a Wigeon. But how could he explain that to Colin?

"Ahh, you're going to do some carving," Colin said. "What will this one be?"

"I'm looking for something that I could carve into a bird," Uri said trying to hide his embarrassment. The last thing he wanted was for his brother to think that he was going soft.

"As a gift for Dinah?" Colin asked.

Uri chuckled; it looked like his brother knew him too well. "A pair of wigeon landed this morning on the river, we discussed them for a while, I thought it might be nice?"

"She will love it." Colin began to take a few logs off the top of the pile and put them in the basket. As he picked up each one he turned it from side to side, reviewing it and letting Uri do the same.

"Stop," Uri said. He reached out and took the piece that Colin had in his hands. It was beautiful, with different colored growth lines through it. They would polish up to perfection. It was deep enough for what he wanted and long enough too. Closing his eyes, he took a deep breath and then opened them to stare at the piece of wood. Gradually, bit by bit, the shape he wished to carve was shown to him. "This one is what I'm looking for."

Colin chuckled. "I don't know how you do it, it looks exactly the same as all the rest to me."

"*Nee*, it is very different, in fact, it is perfect."

"I will leave you to it. Shout at me if you need anything?"

Uri watched Colin walk away. The wood was ideal for what he wanted, but would it make the perfect gift? He had never felt the need to get something right in the way he did right now. It seemed important, and the depth of the importance made him doubt his skills. Would he be able to carve something worthy of Dinah?

***

"You have been very happy this morning," Conrad said.

Dinah realized she had been humming all morning. "I met Uri Phillips this morning while I was out walking," she said. "I invited him to join us for dinner tomorrow night."

Conrad was shaking his head and his eyebrows were drawn down with confusion. "Wasn't it Moses you were courting?"

"*Nee, Daed*, I told you, Moses and I are just friends."

"Is Uri just a friend?"

Dinah knew that a smile had spread across her face. She certainly hoped he wasn't just a friend. "*Nee*, I'm hoping he will be much more. He invited you and me over to the Phillips' farm for Christmas. Obviously, I won't go unless you are well enough."

A smile spread across Conrad's face. "I'm sure I can manage a few hours. If not, you will go. I will not spoil things for you, not anymore."

Dinah reached over and kissed his cheek. "*Daed*, you could never spoil things for me."

CHAPTER EIGHTEEN

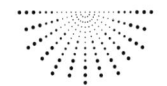

Dinah couldn't keep the smile off her face as she wandered around the marketplace. She was looking for something special for tomorrow's meal, but something that didn't cost too much. Since Leah had left the house, there was less income coming in and she knew they had to make savings. Perhaps, she could even get a job. Mending didn't bring in enough income, not anymore. Only, what could she do? She couldn't leave the house all day, it wouldn't be fair on Conrad.

Two stalls down, she saw Betsy and that was when she had a thought. Perhaps, she could make quilts and sell them at the Phillips' farm as Betsy did. What if they already had too many? Perhaps they didn't need another person to work with them. She knew she could ask Leah, but if she did, Leah might feel obliged to help her. She didn't know Betsy as well as Leah so maybe she would be the perfect person to ask.

"Good day," Leah said as she stepped toward Betsy. However, instead of a friendly smile, the older woman frowned at her and almost turned away. What was wrong?

Betsy's face was pinched, she nodded an acknowledgment and then did turn away.

Dinah couldn't help but notice that she seemed tired and almost downtrodden. As if the weight of the world was on her shoulders. Of course, she was a widow, and with the approaching season of joy... Betsy might miss her husband. Instinctively, Dinah reached out and touched her arm. "Are you all right?"

Betsy turned and her eyes bored into Dinah's. The look was more than unfriendly, it was hostile. Dinah stepped back, and Betsy's eyes softened.

"Have I done something to upset you?" Dinah asked, all thoughts of the job forgotten.

"*Nee*, I just wondered how things were going between you and Moses?" The tone was short and sharp.

Dinah shook her head. "There is nothing between Moses and me. In fact, I'm hoping there will be something between Uri and me. We met this morning…"

Betsy cut her off. "I know what I saw. I won't interrupt your game, however, if you're playing the two brothers against each other that is cruel. But I won't get involved. Now, if you don't mind I have places to be."

Dinah gaped after her wondering exactly what had gone wrong. As she watched, the widow disappeared amongst the crowds and Dinah felt a deep feeling of unrest. If Betsy believed this, then what if Uri found out?

* * *

Leah sat at the dining table in the Phillips' kitchen with a pad and pen in front of her. So far, she had very little on her list.

"You must let me help you more," Ester said.

"*Nee*, you should be resting. I don't know why I'm finding this so hard. After all, it's only a dinner, all I have to do is scale it up."

"Why don't we have a coffee, and then we can think about what we need." Ester rose and crossed to the kettle.

Leah was beside her. "Let me do that, you have worked hard this morning and you should be resting."

"I'm pregnant, I'm not ill." Ester chuckled and shook her head. "You're like a mother hen, clucking around me. I think you're worse than Jeremiah."

"*Nee*, I couldn't be that bad." The two women chuckled as Leah filled the kettle and stoked the stove. "What is wrong with Betsy?"

"I don't know, she said she was not feeling well, but I think it's more than that." Ester shrugged. "I want everything to be wonderful this Christmas and yet it feels like it's falling apart."

"*Nee*, it isn't, we will get it all sorted before the day."

Ester gasped and grabbed for the countertop.

"Are you all right?" Leah asked her.

"I just went a little lightheaded. It's nothing."

Leah shook her head, for she could see that her friend was as white as a sheet. Her face even looked a little clammy. "I'm not having that, let's have you up to bed. Then I will call on Dr. Yoder."

"*Nee,* I will be fine," Ester said, however, she didn't let go of the counter.

Leah fetched a chair and put it next to her. "Take a seat." For a moment she thought that Ester would argue but then her friend nodded and sat down. "Are you feeling any pain?"

"*Nee*, I was just a little lightheaded. I'm sure I will be fine; I don't need the doctor. It is nothing."

"Do you think you can stand?" Leah asked her.

Ester nodded.

"*Gut*, then I will help you up to your bedroom and then, I will explain to Jeremiah what is going on."

For a moment, it looked as if Ester would argue but then she changed her mind and Leah helped her up the stairs. Though her friend still looked pale, she looked better than she had a few moments ago, however, her footsteps seemed a little nervous and she leaned on Leah's arm more than she expected. Hopefully, this was nothing. Just the body adjusting to the stress and strain of pregnancy. Nevertheless, she wasn't prepared to take a chance.

Once she had Ester in bed, she left to talk to Jeremiah. Maybe he wouldn't call the doctor, but perhaps he should call the midwife. Martha Byler would not mind coming out and she would be able to tell if there was any problem.

"Stay here," Leah said and Ester nodded. As she left the room, the sense of worry hung heavy on Leah. *Would her friend be okay?*

* * *

Ester kept a smile on her face until Leah left the room. Taking a few deep breaths, she fought to control the pain and the sense of vertigo that had overwhelmed her. Should she see the midwife? The last thing she wanted to do was cause a panic, and yet, she felt a sense of panic. What if something was wrong with her *boppli*?

Closing her eyes, she started to pray. As the words poured out of her she began to relax. Had this just been caused by worry? In other years, Christmas had been so easy. There was just her and Rhonda and no one else to worry about. Now, she had herself and this *boppli*. Then there was Jeremiah and his brothers, and the three women who were friends. At times, it was all too much. She wanted them all to be happy, to be as happy as her. Was that even possible?

Ester let all of this out in her prayer and as she did she began to feel better. She felt the tension leave her and knew that she would be fine. The sound of heavy footsteps on the stairs jerked her eyes open just as Jeremiah burst into the room. The look of worry on his face filled her heart with love.

"I am fine," she said.

He seemed to arrive at her side on his knees and clasped her hand to his. He kissed it and felt her brow. "Martha is on her way. I'm sure you are fine, but let's be doubly sure."

Leah kissed his hand and smiled. "How could I not be fine with such a wonderful family and friends."

"You are my love and my life. This Christmas is going to be so wonderful; I cannot wait. But, don't you go scaring me like this. My poor heart can't take it." Jeremiah put his hand with hers over his heart.

How could she ever doubt that this Christmas would be anything but wonderful?

CHAPTER NINETEEN

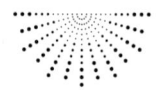

The midwife's grey hair was poking out from her *kapp*. There was a calmness about Martha Byler, she was like your favorite aunt. A little large, probably because everyone gave her cake, but always reassuring. "You'll be fine," Martha said as she picked up her bag.

Ester smiled at the midwife, she was like a comfortable pair of shoes, reliable and trustworthy. Ester felt much better having spoken to her.

"How is Betsy getting on?" Ester asked as the midwife stood at the door. Betsy was a neighbor of Martha and she wondered if she would have any insight into her recent problems.

Martha stopped and looked back. For a moment, a battle crossed her features. It looked like she couldn't decide whether this was something for her to talk about. In the end, she let out a big sigh. "She is struggling, she has fallen for your brother-in-law, Moses and is upset that he is spending time with a younger woman. I know she thinks she is being silly, but the heart will not always obey logic. I think it is worse at this time of year, and because she suffers with her confidence."

Ester let out a breath. She did not believe that Moses was courting, and she was sure that he liked Betsy. *Who was this woman? What was going on?*

"Do you know who it is? For I am sure that Moses likes Betsy."

Martha bit her lower lip. It was not like the confident midwife to be shy. Obviously, she didn't want to speak out of turn.

"Perhaps I can help them if I know who it is," Ester said and pleaded with her eyes for she really did want to help them both. How much she had changed.

"I think it is Dinah Gunden." Martha shrugged.

"Well, that is most strange. For I heard this morning that it is Uri who is courting Dinah." Did he say they were courting? Well, it was close enough and it was clear that that was what he wanted. "Oh, I am so pleased that I am no longer courting. Marriage is much easier."

"That it is," Martha said. "You are fine to get up, just take it easy and call me if you have any more symptoms. I mean that. *Nee* bustling through, if you feel something is wrong get me here, any day, I won't mind."

"*Denke*, I will. Do not worry, I will not tell Betsy that we spoke of this... and if I can help, I will."

* * *

After Ester had reassured Jeremiah that all was fine, he went back to the barn and she made her way down to the kitchen to find Uri and Colin drinking coffee.

"How are you?" They both asked at once.

"I am fine. It was nothing."

"The *boppli*?" Uri asked.

"We are both fine."

"That is great news. Let me make you a drink," Uri said.

Colin was on his feet too. "And I can cut you a slice of cake."

"I am fine, stopped fussing," Ester said as she sat at the table. Within seconds, a cup of coffee and a slice of chocolate cake were put in front of her. "You will have me getting fat." She chuckled but took a bite of the cake anyway.

Both of the brothers were sitting at the table but there was something about Uri that was different. He was like the proverbial cat on a hot tin roof. The smile on his face was broader than normal, he was almost glowing as much as she was. "What is it?" she asked him.

Uri blushed but said nothing.

"He's happy because he is courting," Colin said.

"*Ack*, of course, Dinah. You invited her for Christmas and are having dinner with her. That is really *gut* news and I'm so happy for you." Happy but curious. Why did Betsy think that Dinah was courting Moses? She must ask, but who, Uri... it could ruin his happiness, perhaps Moses?

"*Denke*, I have to get back to my carving," Uri said and grabbed himself a coffee before almost running from the room.

"Are you really all right?" Colin asked. "If there's anything I can do to help, you must let me know."

Ester reached across the table and touched his hand. "I am fine. However, I wish this little one would stop kicking and hurry up and get here."

"Be careful what you wish for," Colin said and raised his eyebrows.

"How are you settling in?" Ester asked, still trying to work out how she could help her friend.

"It has been better than I expected," Colin said but he lowered his eyes to the table as if he did not want to hold her gaze.

"Jeremiah will come around," she said. "He loves you very much, he's just cautious. The longer you stay here, the more he will trust you. Do not worry, the rest of us trust you."

Moses wandered into the kitchen; unlike Uri, he looked sad, as if he had the weight of the world on his shoulders.

"What is it?" Ester asked hoping that this might be her chance.

"It's nothing," Moses said and was about to walk out of the room with a coffee.

"I'm not believing that one bit." Ester pointed at a chair. "Take a seat, and let's talk about this."

Moses sat down and held his coffee in front of him, like a shield.

"Smile, brother," Colin said. "It looks like our plan has worked, Dinah and Uri are on the verge of happiness."

What plan was this, Ester thought?

Moses, however, didn't smile' in fact, he looked even sadder.

"What is it?" Ester asked.

Moses took a sip of his coffee and for a moment she thought he wouldn't answer but then he looked up with almost despair in his eyes. "You know Betsy, I really like her but she has turned away from me. She will not even talk to me."

"Do not worry," Colin said. "I have already got Uri and Dinah together; my next project will be you and Betsy."

Moses drank his coffee in one go and almost slammed the cup back down on the table. "I think you've done enough." With that, Moses left the room.

"What did I do?" Colin asked.

"Has Moses spent any time with Dinah? I know he sat with her at the dinner, has he been courting her?"

"Well, not really spent time with her, just a dinner or two at their house," Colin said while staring at his hands.

"Why would he do that? I believe that Betsy's heart is hurt because of this."

Colin put his hands to his head. "Oh, *nee*... I believe this is my fault. I just wanted my brothers to be happy, especially as we're close to Christmas. I thought that Moses could let Dinah know that Uri liked her. However, I think I may have made things worse. Now, I need to work out how to solve the problem."

"I know you only meant well, but the truth is always the right answer," Ester said. "Explain it to me, what happened?"

Colin explained his plan, how Moses spoke to Dinah to tell her that Uri liked her and to encourage her to talk to him and to give him a chance.

Ester sighed, it hurt her to see Colin and Moses suffering so as well as Betsy. What a mess they had made! Maybe she could talk to Betsy and explain that this was all just a silly mistake.

CHAPTER TWENTY

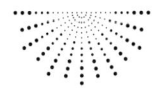

"How are you enjoying the meal?" Conrad asked.

Uri chewed quickly and swallowed his food. A big smile was on his face. "It is delicious. Dinah is an excellent cook."

Color flooded Dinah's cheeks and she shook her head. "It is just a chicken, and a few vegetables. Nothing to write home about, I'm sure."

Conrad shook his head. "*Nee*, you run yourself down, daughter. Your chicken is always moist and beautifully flavored. And these beans, the butter just makes them so delicious."

"So that is what it is," Uri said. "They really are lovely."

"Stop it, both of you," Dinah said. "The meal is fine, but it is nothing at all special. However, I did make a blackberry and apple crumble that you might like.

"I can't wait," Uri said.

Conrad was looking well but she knew it could change so quickly. He was having a *gut* day and he was so happy to have some company and no doubt to see her smile. As she cleared the plates, he looked on at her with pride in his eyes.

"It is some time since I've seen my daughter so happy," Conrad said.

"I'm pleased to hear that," Uri said. "I never wanted to make someone as happy as I want to make her happy."

Dinah came back to the table carrying dishes of the crumble. She handed them out and then sat down. Looking around the table as the conversation seemed to come to a halt. "Were you talking about me?"

"We were, but it was all *gut*," Conrad said. "I like this man; he can come anytime."

"*Denke*," Uri said. "I hope you will be able to join us on Christmas Day."

"I hope so too," Conrad said. "But if I can't, you must make sure that my daughter goes anyway. I do not wish to spoil her life. Not anymore."

"*Daed*, you have never spoiled my life. I have loved looking after you."

"And yes, with Leah gone, times are hard. A*ck*... look at me, the old man spoiling things. We will manage, we always do and as always, Bishop Beiler will look after us."

Dinah hoped that this was right, however, since Leah had gone the family finances were not doing well. She had to find a way to make ends meet. A way that would not make her father feel like a burden. If only there wasn't a problem between her and Betsy, making quilts would be perfect for her.

* * *

Uri walked back to the farm to find his brother, Jeremiah still in the barn. "What are you doing out here this late?"

"I was just finishing this," Jeremiah said and pulled back a sheet to reveal a crib. It was beautifully carved, and a real work of art.

"That is wonderful," Uri said.

"I wanted it to be special, I really hope it is," Jeremiah said. Though he knew he was *gut* at carving, he also knew he was not as *gut* as Uri. For a moment, he wondered why he hadn't asked his brother to help.

Uri was inspecting the woodwork. On the head and foot of the crib, Jeremiah had carved leaves and acorns, and flowers. They were okay, but were they as *gut* as Uri could've done?

"This is wonderful work," Uri said. "You are getting so much better."

"*Denke*, I was worried if you would think it was *gut* enough, or not."

"It is, it is wonderful."

"How was your evening?" Jeremiah asked, and he felt pleased that his brother blushed a little.

"I think that Dinah and I are courting properly. I wasn't sure at first, but Conrad really likes me, or at least he says he does. I can't explain how happy I feel. It's like I just want to shout it from the rooftops."

Jeremiah patted him on the back. "You do not have to explain it to me. I am still so in love with Ester that I totally understand. I'm really pleased you two are getting on so well."

"*Denke*, can I help you with this?" Uri asked looking away to hide the color on his cheeks.

"*Nee*, you get in and get warm. I'm nearly finished off here."

"*Gut* night." Uri walked out of the barn.

Jeremiah replaced a sheet over the crib and was tidying up his tools when Colin walked into the barn looking most despondent.

"Can I have a moment of your time?" Colin asked.

"Of course, it is chilly here, do you want to talk in the house?" Jeremiah felt his heart stumble, was his brother about to let them down? Was he about to leave just before Christmas?

"*Nee*, I would like to do it here… I'm not quite sure what to say." Colin had his hands clasped before him and he was finding it hard to hold Jeremiah's eyes. This was not like him, Jeremiah was worried. A feeling of despondency came over him, he had been right all along. Colin was going to break all their hearts. Still, he had to try and help his brother. He reached out to touch his shoulder just as Abraham ran into the barn.

"Ester is calling for help," Abraham said.

Everything was forgotten as Jeremiah ran from the barn. As he made his way across the snowy yard he whispered a prayer for his *fraa* and unborn *boppli*. Fear sliced into his stomach as the worse possible scenario came into his mind. Would he lose them both?

CHAPTER TWENTY-ONE

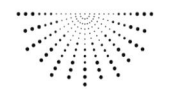

*J*eremiah ran from the barn and across the open land toward the house. His heart was in his throat and fear curled in his stomach like a snake ready to strike. As his feet caught a patch of ice, he started to slip and wheeled his arms, willing himself forward for he could not waste the time to fall. Righting himself, he pushed even faster, up the steps and through the door.

Through the living room door, he could see Leah standing over Ester. The look on her face was enough to stop his heart but he kept moving forward. Hopefully, Abraham would've gone for the doctor. "Ester, Ester, my darling, how are you?" He stopped at her side.

It was worse than he thought, Ester was lying on the sofa, pale and breathing so fast that she must be in labor. It was too soon. What should he do? He took her hand. "Is the *boppli* coming?"

Colin had arrived at his side. "Ester, look at me," he said.

Jeremiah wanted to shove his meddling brother aside, but it was actually Colin who moved him aside and came to stand next to his *fraa*. Though he wanted to move, though he wanted to pull him away, Jeremiah found that he was frozen to the spot. He looked around to see Abraham standing at the door and he wanted to tell him to run for Dr. Yoder but the words froze in his throat as he heard Colin speaking.

"Look at me," Colin said. "I want you to take a breath at the same time as I do, breathing with me. Breathe in, one, two, three, four, five," Colin counted as he breathed in. "Now breathe out with me one, two, three, four, five. Keep this up, breathe with me. One, two, three, four, five."

Jeremiah wanted to scream. Why was his brother just counting and telling Ester to breathe? It made no sense. He turned and grabbed hold of Abraham. "Why haven't you gone for the doctor?" Abraham was shaking his head and pointing over his shoulder. Jeremiah let go, ashamed that he had manhandled his brother, and turned back to Ester expecting to find her deep in labor, but instead, she looked much better.

"You are doing great," Colin said.

"What happened to me?" Ester asked and although she was slightly breathless she was looking much more like her normal self.

"I think you had a panic attack," Colin said.

"A panic attack?" Ester asked. "But it felt so terrible. I thought I was going to die, I thought I was going to lose the *boppli*."

"*Nee*, you will be fine," Colin said.

Jeremiah came across to Ester and dropped to his knees, he took her hand in his and brought it to his lips. "How are you?"

"I am fine, whatever it was, it is gone now," Ester said and she raised her head to Colin. "*Denke*, I do not know what I would have done if you were not here."

"It is fine, I have seen this before. Now, I will leave you two alone." Colin took Abraham by the arm and led him out of the room, closing the door behind him.

The door opened and Jeremiah came out. "I want to say *denke* too. Where did you learn about this?"

"It was on my travels," Colin said and Jeremiah could see that he was expecting to get into trouble for saying such a thing.

"Well, I am glad that you spent time out of our district. What you did for Ester tonight, I cannot say *denke* enough. You said it was a panic attack, I do not understand."

"When someone is under a lot of stress, the body can think there is danger. It makes you hyperventilate, or have a panic attack," Colin said.

"I am so pleased you are here," Jeremiah said.

"*Denke*," Colin hung his head, "but, I fear I may have created a problem with our brothers when all I wished to do was help."

"That does not matter now, Ester is fine, we will deal with any other problems tomorrow. Do you think we need to call Dr. Yoder?"

"*Nee*, Ester will be fine. If it happens again, you saw what I did, that will help her... but it will be best if she has no stress."

Jeremiah went back into the living room but Colin knew this was all his fault. Ester would be panicking over Christmas, and about why Moses was so unhappy. He hated himself for causing such problems and wondered if he would've been better never coming home.

***

"*Gut* day," Uri said as he came into the small house the following morning to see Dinah working on the meal.

Should he tell her about Ester? His brothers had told him that it was nothing to worry about but before he could decide she was speaking.

"It is *gut* to see you," Dinah said. "Take off your hat and coat and make yourself at home."

"What is it?" Uri asked for she seemed stressed and tired, was it him?

"I'm sorry, my *daed* is not as *gut* today. I'm wondering if I will make it to your place for Christmas." She turned from him and began to serve up the vegetables.

"It doesn't matter if you don't make it, I will come here. Is there anything I can do for your *daed*?"

Dinah shook her head. "There is nothing, he has his medicine, but there is nothing more the doctors can do."

"Would you rather be alone?" Uri asked, though he had his fingers crossed behind his back, he prayed that she didn't say *jah*. How strange was this, at one time he would've shied away from such a responsibility? However, now, he really wanted to help.

"*Nee*, it would be nice to have some company. I'm sure my *daed* will enjoy it too. Go on through, I will be there in a minute."

"Let me help you," he said and picked up one of the dishes of vegetables to carry them through to the dining table. Conrad was sitting in his wheelchair. In many ways, he looked just as he had the day before. However, his eyes were not as bright and he was nowhere near as cheery. It was almost as if he didn't realize that Uri was there.

The meal was simple but delicious, however, Conrad did not engage in the conversation and Uri was finding it hard to talk to Dinah. It was obvious that she was worried. How he wished there was some way that he could ease her strain.

"Let me get the dessert," Dinah said.

As she left the room Conrad seemed to stare at Uri. There was a look of confusion in his eyes and he wondered if he should call her back. "Are you all right, Conrad?"

"I was wondering why you were here instead of your brother?" Conrad said.

Uri was both confused and startled at such a statement. What would his brother have been doing here?

CHAPTER TWENTY-TWO

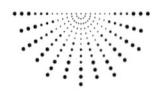

Dinah put a shoofly pie on the table and Conrad looked at her and shook his head. "What is happening?"

"What do you mean, *Daed*?"

"What happened to the other one?" Conrad asked.

"He's not here today," Dinah said.

"Who is the other one, who else have you been courting?" Uri asked a little too sharply. Suddenly, the food was not sitting well in his stomach. He knew there was nothing wrong with the food, but who had she been courting?

"It's not like it sounds," Dinah said. "Moses came around to see me and had dinner with me and my *daed* once or twice."

Uri felt a flood of fury rush through his veins. What was going on? "You were courting my brother?"

Dinah flushed and shook her head. "N*ee*, it is not like that. Moses simply came… well, he came… to explain to me that you liked me. He was here to try and help get us together."

"That makes no sense at all, do you prefer his company?"

Dinah shook her head, and he could see the concern in her eyes so why did it hurt so much? "I did not prefer your brother at all, I was so pleased when you and I got talking…"

"And yet you had dinner with him twice, or was it more than twice?"

Dinah opened her mouth to say something when there was a knock at the door. She rose to answer it to find Colin and Jeremiah there. What was going on?

Soon the brothers were all back in the dining room. "Should I make some coffee?" Dinah asked.

"Now there are more brothers," Conrad said, "but where is the other one, the one who came before, I liked him."

"He's not here today, *Daed*," Dinah said. "What are you all doing here?"

"I fear that I may have caused the problem," Colin said. "I wanted to help my brother. I guess it was a way to prove I was worthy to be back... but I think I have just made more of a problem."

"Will someone explain to me what is going on?" Uri asked.

"I'm tired, I want to go to my room," Conrad said.

"It's all right, I will take you." Dinah wheeled him out of the room and into the bedroom. When she had closed the door she leaned against it and closed her eyes. What was going on?.

"I like the other one," Conrad said as she got him ready for bed. "Is this one messing you about?"

"Moses was just a friend," Dinah said. "I like Uri, you need to rest now, you know you mustn't get stressed."

Conrad laid back on the bed and closed his eyes. Dinah kissed his cheek and whispered a little prayer. She just hoped that she hadn't messed things up.

When Dinah came out of the bedroom she could hear Colin explaining his plan to Uri. How he had felt as if he was an outsider and how he wished to bring Uri and Dinah together. She could see the fury and the hurt in Uri's eyes and she wished she had never got involved in this scheme. Why couldn't Uri have just told her how he felt in the first place. It would've made things so much easier.

"So, you went behind my back?" Uri asked. "You talked about me and schemed without telling me what you were doing?"

Dinah couldn't decide whether Uri was angry with her or Colin, for his eyes were flicking from one to the other. The hurt on his face was obvious. What could she do to stop this?

"Does it make any difference?" Dinah asked.

The look on Uri's face told her that it did. She did not think that he would ever forgive her and yet had she really done anything wrong? Suddenly, she felt so tired. Tired and lonely and defeated. For a moment she had thought that she could have a normal life. But she had been fooled, the excitement had been too much for her *daed* and now he was back to confused and exhausted. She had been selfish and she was better to let this go and to carry on as things were before.

The brothers were still arguing, but she could no longer hear what they were saying, there was just a buzzing of panic in her mind. "My *daed* is not well, you all need to leave."

The talking stopped and the room was instantly silent. Uri was looking at her, pleading with his eyes. But it was too late, she had made up her mind, she was best on her own. "Go, I do not wish to be involved in any of this. Just leave me and my *daed* alone."

"This is all my fault," Colin said. "We will go now, but we are here if you need anything, and do not blame Uri for my foolishness."

Dinah could not bear to hear anymore, she turned and walked out of the room hoping that they would leave of their own accord.

CHAPTER TWENTY-THREE

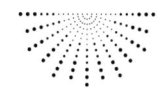

It was Christmas Eve morning and Dinah had been awake for hours. It was snowing gently outside. It was the light and fluffy snow that was pleasant to watch and fun to walk in. Many times, she stared out of the window and thought about going for a walk. *Would she meet Uri? Could they talk? Was this anger she felt foolish, for, after all, she had gone along with the plan? Why were things so complicated?*

It would soon be time for Conrad to wake and she realized she had missed her chance. If she had been going to leave the house, she needed to do it before now. Never mind, maybe there would be another chance. A dark fog seemed to descend over her, it felt as if she had missed her chance as if this was her life now. That made her feel worse, for she loved her life and didn't resent it one bit. She cared for her *daed* and mended clothes for others. That kept her going, kept them going, what more did she need?

Love!

But love was not for the likes of her.

Even as she pushed the thought away she knew it was too late, she was already in love with Uri. Was it too soon? Could it happen like that? It didn't matter for she had lost her chance.

Tears formed at the back of her eyes but she bit them down and put the kettle back on the hotspot of the stove. This morning's breakfast was a Christmas breakfast casserole. She had managed to get a little turkey meat and some Brussels sprouts and had fried them up and added them to the egg and cheese mixture that her *daed* loved so much. At one time, she had planned to save this for Christmas morning. Would they still be welcome at the Phillips' farm? It was all so difficult.

If they didn't go, then was she being petulant? If they did go, and they were no longer welcome... it didn't bear thinking about. The disappointment for her *daed* would be too much. Would he even be well enough to go?

The casserole was almost ready and so was the coffee when she heard Conrad stir so she made her way to his room. The breakfast was on the warming plate and it would be ready as soon as he was. Putting a big smile on her face she walked into the room. "*Gut* morning." The words froze in her throat. He was not looking well this morning.

"*Gut* morning, dear."

Conrad was much weaker than yesterday but she eased him up on the bed and packed cushions behind him. Once he was washed and comfortable she fetched the breakfast through and sat in the chair next to the bed. Though he smiled and tried to talk, he could hardly eat much at all. Perhaps she should make some soup?

"Would you like to sleep?" she asked.

"I am worried about what is happening," he said, his voice much quieter than normal.

"There is nothing to worry about, *Daed*," she said, trying to soothe him and hoping he would go back to sleep. It looked like he needed the rest.

"You need to understand what is happening." He reached out to take her hand but his grip was weak. "The Phillips brothers are flawed. If they play each other off like that... I do not think you should be with them. Find a better man." As he finished talking, his eyes closed and she thought he had fallen asleep.

"I will, *Daed*," she whispered, and yet, she didn't want to. In bed last night she had tossed and turned and prayed. All the time, she had wondered if there was still a chance at happiness with Uri. There was something about him that made her feel... complete. Should she go to them for Christmas, was there a chance of happiness?

On the bed, Conrad started to cough, and before Dinah could stand, it had turned into a seizure. Though this had happened before, and she knew what to do, panic still raced through her. For a moment, she froze, and wondered if she had caused this? Christmas was forgotten, all she cared about was that her *daed* would survive.

* * *

Uri had not gone for his walk, but instead, he had sat in the barn watching the snow fall all around him. It was beautiful, a magnificent display of *Gott's* glory, and normally it would have delighted him. However, his heart was heavy and all he could think about was Dinah. Why had he gotten so angry? Neither she nor his brothers had meant any harm.

"I brought you a coffee," Colin said as he walked into the barn with Moses at his side.

"We never meant to cause any harm," Moses said.

"How is Ester?" Uri asked.

"She's fine," Colin said. "Jeremiah was going to spend some time with her this morning, so we said we would look after the animals and do any jobs that needed doing. That also means that you are free... if you have anywhere you need to be!"

"I don't, really," Uri said, and yet he wanted to say *denke* and run from the barn all the way to Dinah's house.

"I only wanted to help," Colin said. "I know I have messed up big style, I think, for both of you," he looked at Moses, "but I really did only want to help."

"It is all right," Uri said. "I don't blame you, but I understand that Dinah was angry. She will not want to talk to me now."

"Why not?" Moses asked.

Uri's eyes opened wide with hope but then he shrugged. "Because I was a fool, I messed up, I was angry at you in her *daed's* house. What must she think of me, what must he think of me?"

"That you're a bit of an idiot, just the same as we think," Moses said with a big grin on his face.

"With brothers like you, who needs enemies," Uri said but a grin had formed on his face.

"Moses is right," Colin said. "Though what I did, I did with a *gut* heart and for *gut* reasons, it was wrong. What I should've done, was talk to you and told you to talk to Dinah. All you needed to do was tell her how you feel and none of this needed to happen. I think that both of you can sort out these problems if you just do that. Go, now, and talk to the women you love. Tell them how you feel and let us enjoy Christmas as a family."

Moses shook his head. "I do not think I can do this, not now, not yet."

"We will help you," Uri said, getting to his feet. "But right now, I have somewhere I need to be... and some things I need to say. Wish me luck, brothers, for I feel I will need it."

As the brothers wished him luck, he set out into the snow with a smile on his face and hope in his heart. He prayed as he walked, for if she didn't forgive him, he did not know what he would do.

CHAPTER TWENTY-FOUR

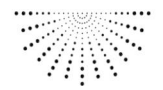

On the bed, Conrad's muscles tensed and relaxed as his seizure continued. His thrashing was so violent that she was unable to turn him onto his side. That was normally all she could do. He had taken his medication and the doctor had told her that they simply had to let these seizures ride out.

She tried to duck under his arms to turn him, in her mind he was gasping for breath, but she wasn't sure if that was panic or if it was actually happening. One of his hands struck her face and she moved back with a grunt. She knew he didn't mean it, what was wrong with her, why couldn't she do this?

The sound of a knock on the door made her jump and she let out a yelp. Could it be the doctor? Conrad was still seizing, and for a moment, she thought about ignoring the door, but perhaps it was someone who could help?

As she opened the door she saw Uri in front of her, he opened his mouth and she knew he was talking but she couldn't hear a thing. All she could think about was her father and getting him onto his side. She grabbed Uri by the hand and dragged him through to her father's room. "Help me, I need to turn him."

Uri was both taller and stronger than her and he grasped Conrad's arms pinning them down by his side and eased him over onto his side. It helped, he was breathing easier and the seizure was not quite so violent.

Dinah quickly checked his airways, they were clear and she let out a sigh of relief, however, the seizure continued.

Uri stood in front of the bed but left Conrad as he was. Dinah knew this was the right thing to do. To stand there, to make sure he did not fall out of bed, but to do nothing other than keep his airways clear. That was what she had always been told. However, this was the longest seizure he had had and she felt overwhelmed and unsure of what to do.

"It is all right," Uri said. "This will pass, let us pray."

Dinah looked up at him and felt tears flood her eyes. She knew he was right, that they must trust in *Gott* to bring her father back, but it was so hard. She hated to see him like this, and the thought of losing him was like a dagger to her heart. What would she do? Suddenly, all thoughts of Christmas were forgotten, all that mattered was that he made it through this day.

"Do you need me to fetch Dr. Yoder?" Uri asked.

"*Nee*, I do not think so, perhaps we will get him to check, later." Dinah felt as if she was making no sense. Part of her wanted to shout *jah*, for to do anything was better than doing nothing. But she knew that the doctor could do nothing, and by the time Uri had fetched him the seizure would be over. *Nee*, she needed him here, she needed his support.

Uri reached across the bed and took her hand in his. "Let us pray," he said as he closed his eyes and began to pray for Conrad's recovery.

At first, Dinah couldn't join in. The panic was like a ball in her throat, it was lodged there making it impossible to breathe and even to think. However, as she watched Uri, so calm and confident, she started to relax. The seizure was easing and she began to pray.

Almost instantly, Conrad relaxed back on the bed. His eyes flickered open and he nodded to her. Though he couldn't talk, just yet, she realized that he was fine. "*Denke, Gott*," she whispered. "Sleep now, *Daed,* all is fine."

Conrad nodded and closed his eyes and it seemed as if he had fallen into a sleep. Dinah let out a big breath of air and turned to Uri, realizing that he was still holding her hand, she let it go. "*Denke*, I do not know what I would've done if you had not arrived."

"It is nothing, I had an uncle, many years ago who suffered seizures. How are you doing?"

"I could drink a coffee," she said and managed a smile.

"Your wish is my command. Do you want to stay here, I will find things and bring them to you?"

Dinah took one look at her father and could see that he was sleeping peacefully. The seizure had probably been no worse than others. She had simply felt more panicked. Instead of handling it, she had let her panic take over and she wondered why she had done that. The danger was over, she didn't need to call the doctor, and she knew he would sleep now for a few hours. "*Nee*, he will be fine. I think I panicked."

She led Uri into the kitchen and started to fill the kettle. However, her hands were shaking and he took it off her. The feel of his fingers on her hand was warm and comforting and for a moment she wanted to lean back against his chest and close her eyes. However, he moved away and put the kettle on the stove.

"Sit," he said as he took a poker and gave the fire in the stove a stir. "I can manage this."

Uri made the coffee and came to the table sitting across from her. The silence was growing between them, but Dinah looked out the window at the falling snow. Just at that moment, the sun broke through the clouds and sent a ray of glorious light into the kitchen. She felt blessed. Conrad had survived, Christmas was nearly here, and nothing else mattered.

As she looked across the table, she could see that Uri was unsure of himself. Should she tell him it was fine, should she try to talk to him, or had he come here to tell her that the invitation for Christmas Day was rescinded?

CHAPTER TWENTY-FIVE

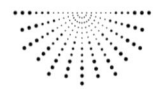

Dinah felt a lump in her throat, she wanted to talk, she wanted Uri to talk, but nothing came out. Looking at her coffee, she picked up the cup and took a sip. Ouch, it was hot, but what had she expected?

Uri cleared his throat, and Dinah looked up at him, her eyes wide and expectant. However, he simply looked down at the table and his hands clasped together. It was clear that he wanted nothing to do with her. That was why he had come, to tell her it was over... had it ever started?

"*Denke*," she said. "My *daed* will be fine now, I understand that you are angry with me. I understand if we can't be friends anymore. You do not need to feel you must stay."

Uri shook his head and there was a worried look in his eyes. "That is not what I meant. I did not mean to get angry at you or my brother, I was just shocked. I thought that our meeting on the river bank was... destined... or something, it was silly."

"*Nee*, I must take some of the blame. When your brother came to me, I was so excited that I went along with it. I guess, well, I guess I never thought it through and I'm sorry for that. I also enjoyed Moses's company. There was never any thought of courting him, but it was nice to talk to someone else. It was nice to see my *daed* with a smile on his face. He rarely gets to speak to anyone but me and of course, Bishop and Sarah Beiler come visiting. I don't know what I would do without them."

"I should not jump to conclusions," he said.

Tears ran from Dinah's eyes and down her face.

"What is it, I am so sorry, what have I done?" Uri asked.

"It is not you. I worry that the potential loss of my father was my punishment for not being honest with you. If only I had just talked to you."

Uri reached across the table and put his hands over hers. "*Nee*, it is not, of course, it is not. There is no fault on your part, you did nothing wrong. I spoke to Colin, and to Moses and all they did was talk to you about the fact that I liked you. I am the one who is unworthy, I felt it before, which was why I could never talk to you. I feel it now, for losing my temper when everyone was trying to help me."

"*Nee*, you are not unworthy, you have never been unworthy. You appeared just as I needed you and the help you gave me with calming my *daed*, I will never forget that. I would like to talk to you again, where do we go from here? Might we find a way to start over?"

Uri smiled and kept his hands on hers. "With the approach of Christmas, anything is possible." He stood up and leaned across the table planting a kiss on her cheek.

Diana felt as if her heart had been lifted and all its burdens removed. She could feel the heat in her cheeks and knew she must be blushing. This was her first kiss. But there was one thing that she still wanted - if it could be possible. "Is the invitation to Christmas lunch still open?" Just as she said the words she realized that it was more than likely that her *daed* would not be up for it.

They had no food in, and nothing to make Christmas special. He would be so disappointed. Though she had made a few paper chains and pulled some holly from the hedge, the house looked much as it did all year long. If she didn't go to the Phillips', they would have no Christmas.

"Of course, it is still open to you both. However, there is more than enough food, and with all you have going on would it be better if I brought a bit of Christmas to you both here?"

Dinah knew that she was grinning so wide that she felt her cheeks might split. "I cannot think of anything better. Please, understand that we do not have much and I am sorry if it is not up to the standards that you would like." What did they have, what could she make? Maybe, she could ask the bishop to loan her some food?

"I do not want to say the wrong thing, but we have plenty. I would love it if you could share it with us. I can bring food and decorations. I understand that you were coming to us so would have nothing in. It is nothing to be ashamed of."

Dinah stood up and walked around the table to find him standing too. She reached up on her tiptoes and kissed him on the cheek. He put his arms around her and held her tightly before placing a quick and tender kiss on her lips.

This was going to be the best Christmas ever. Dinah couldn't wait until tomorrow.

* * *

Uri arrived back at the small house less than an hour after he had left. This time he had brought a buggy and the horse was sheltering under a tree with a rug on and hay for it to eat. He carried in box after box. The first was filled with food. Such a wonderful amount of food that Dinah felt her eyes flood with tears. Then he brought in a Christmas tree and tinsel and bits to decorate it with. There were chocolate baubles, cookies, and homemade decorations.

Together they made the house look much more festive, with candles in the windows and the tree in the corner, and paperchains from the ceiling. They added it to the holly that she had already put up and once they were finished they stood back.

"It is perfect," Dinah said. "*Denke* so much."

"I have enjoyed it so much; I wish I could stay but I still have things to do. I will see you tomorrow."

Dinah squeezed his hand before walking him to the door. Before she opened it she reached up and kissed his cheek. "Happy Christmas."

"Happy Christmas to you too. I know it will be my happiest yet."

Dinah felt her heart flutter as he walked away. How could she have been so lucky?

* * *

It was Christmas morning, and Dinah wasn't expecting Uri until later. First, he would attend the service with his family. She wished that she could go, but she wasn't comfortable leaving her father alone just yet. She knew that Bishop Beiler would understand and with joy she looked around the kitchen.

The previous evening, Uri had come back with the decorations and food. It still made her feel so lucky, so loved? *Jah,* though she knew it was too soon, she did feel loved.

She closed her eyes and remembered how wonderful it had been. They laughed as they decorated the house. Was this what it was like to be part of a family? She knew that she must not get overexcited. That she must not read more into this than was there. After all, they were only courting.

However, she had put on her best dress and found herself twirling around the kitchen and the room looking at the wonderful decorations and the tree that Uri had brought. Her heart was singing with joy.

"What has made you so happy?" Conrad called from his room.

"I didn't realize you were awake just yet. How are you feeling?" she said as she went through to him.

"I am much better, and I think I have Uri to thank for helping me."

"*Ack*, he just happened to be here. And he's coming later, I hope that is all right?" Dinah could see that he was feeling much better, his speech was stronger, and there was color in his cheeks and a smile on his face.

"It is fine, why don't you go to service?"

"*Nee, Daed*, it is some distance today and I do not wish to leave you." She hid her disappointment well for she would've loved to have gone. However, with the snow on the ground and no horse, it was a long journey. The last thing she wanted to do was leave, let alone for all that time.

Before she could say anymore, there was a knock on the door. Glancing through the windows she could see a buggy and she recognized it was one of the Phillips brother's horses. Surely, it was too early for Uri to be here, and why had he come in the buggy? Had something gone wrong?

A spike of adrenaline raised the hairs on her neck, she did not think she could take any more disappointments.

CHAPTER TWENTY-SIX

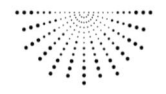

When Dinah opened the door she was surprised to find both Uri and Moses. Had the brothers come to apologize again?

"*Gut* morning," they both said. "How is your *daed*?" Uri asked.

"*Gut* morning. He's doing well, but still a little weak. I think I would prefer to stay here rather than come to the farm. I don't want to spoil things for anyone, you do not have to stay with me. The things you brought have already made our Christmas and I know you would want to be with your family."

Uri smiled. "I will be here, I can't wait. I have a surprise for you, if you would like to come to service with me, Moses has offered to stay with Conrad."

Moses was nodding and smiling at this. "I enjoyed speaking to him, and I know the bishop won't mind me missing the service if he knows it's for a *gut* cause."

Dinah was torn between the joy of accepting and the worry of putting her burden on someone else.

"You're thinking too much," Uri said. "It is settled, Moses will enjoy it, grab your coat and let's go."

Dinah could not believe the change in him. His confidence was so much better and Moses was chuckling, obviously thinking the same. Quickly, she went and told Conrad what was happening. He was over the moon that she could go, and happy to spend the morning talking with Moses.

When she was in the buggy she turned to Uri once more. "I cannot say *denke* enough for this."

"It is Christmas, and I would much rather be with you than with Moses." He chuckled to let her know that he was kind of teasing.

Soon, the horse was trotting along the lane. It was so beautiful. Every branch was coated with snow, and the fields and houses were painted with it. It was almost too bright for the eyes, but she could not stop staring with the biggest smile on her face. She couldn't remember a better Christmas.

What would people think when she arrived with Uri? Once more her face burned with heat. They would know that they were courting. Did this make it official?

"I have wanted to ask to drive you to service for some time," he said as if reading her thoughts. "I would like it very much if I could do this for every service if that is all right with you?"

"I can think of nothing I would like more," she said.

Uri slowed the horse and pointed at a tree in the hedge line. "Look, there is often a pair of birds in this tree."

Dinah could see a beautiful tufted red bird sitting on the snow-covered branches and next to it was a slightly smaller pale brown almost yellowish bird with a tinge of red to its tufted head and wings. "They are beautiful, what are they?"

"They are northern red cardinals. Their plumage stays like this all year round. It makes them look magnificent against the bleak black of the snow-covered branches. Listen, it is the female that sings as much as the male."

Dinah could hear the sweet, sweet, sweet, cheer, cheer, cheer sound that the birds were making. It brought a smile to her lips. "What else do you know about them?" She asked.

"Don't go teasing me, I could talk about this all day and we will end up late for service and you will be bored with me."

"I want to learn, I see them all the time, but I never really looked. Please tell me more."

A big smile came over Uri's face as he began to tell her about the birds while driving the horse along the road. "As I said, the female sings as well as the male, and they often sing for a long time. The male birds are very good *daeds*. They will protect their nest with their lives and are dedicated to their offspring and good providers. However, they are also quite aggressive and a little silly! Both the males and females will be seen fighting their own reflection in a window or a mirror. I think they might have anger issues."

Dinah chuckled at the image that was brought to her mind.

As they drove along, he told her more and more about the birds and Dinah found she was fascinated. She had seen these feathered beauties all her life but had never thought much about them. Now, she could understand why he was so intrigued and she wanted to learn more.

The service was wonderful, it was the first time in a few years that she had been able to attend the Christmas service and it was full of cheer and good hope, and well wishes. But soon, they were in the buggy on the way back and she found herself worried about her *daed*. Was he all right?

"Do not worry, he will be fine. My brother can be responsible at times," Uri said with a chuckle.

That was when Dinah realized that he had taken the wrong road and he was heading up to a hill that looked down over the river. "Where are we going?"

"It is just a small detour; are you warm enough?"

"I am, this blanket you brought is wonderful and we have only just finished a hot chocolate at the service." She couldn't help but think that he looked nervous and she was starting to worry.

Within just a couple of minutes, he turned the buggy around at the top of the hill and parked up with them facing down toward the river. It was snowing softly and it gave the air a festive feel.

Slowly, he turned to her and took her hands in his. "I know that we have not been courting long, but I feel... I feel something I've never felt before. Dinah, I love you."

For a moment she was not sure what to say. Was it too soon? How did she feel? Before she could even answer these questions herself, her mouth opened. "I love you too," she said.

"I know it is so sudden, and I know I haven't asked your *daed*, but would you, maybe, sometime next year, would you marry me?"

Tears flooded from her eyes and she shook her head to clear them.

"I'm sorry, it was too soon. I've messed things up again," he said. "Please don't hold this against me, we can go as slow as you like."

Dinah was still shaking her head but she couldn't get the words out so she leaned forward and took his hands in hers and placed a kiss against his lips. "I love you, and I cannot wait to marry you, you have made this the happiest Christmas ever."

He pulled her into his arms and she melted against him. There was such a feeling of warmth and belonging in her heart, it was the true spirit of Christmas.

As they drove back to her small house, holding hands, Dinah could not help but give thanks for her Christmas blessing.

CHAPTER TWENTY-SEVEN

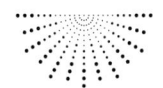

In the kitchen of the Phillips' farmhouse, Leah was busily preparing the lunch. There was a turkey in the oven along with vegetables and potatoes. She had prepared a ham pot pie and noodles for those who wanted something different. There was also a rhubarb custard pie which she knew was Abraham's favorite. As the house filled up she felt her heart begin to flutter. Could she manage this? What if it all went wrong?

The sound of the door opening had her turning and almost dropping the dish she was holding.

"It's only me," Abraham said. "I came to see if you needed any help?"

Leah swallowed down her panic, and closed her eyes, she could do this. "I think I'm fine."

"That didn't sound very convincing, come here." He took the dish off her and put it on the surface and pulled the oven gloves off her hands. Then he pulled her into his arms and held her against his chest. "Everything smells fantastic, and you are doing a great job. Why don't you come through and relax for a while? We are about to start handing out the gifts."

Leah nodded. She could not imagine what he had gotten her for Christmas. And she wondered if the gift she had got him would be inadequate. Why was she finding this so stressful?

"Have you heard from Dinah?" Abraham asked.

"At the service, she was looking happy and I think Uri will look after her. She can't get over today, I will go and see her tomorrow."

"That sounds like a wonderful plan." He kissed her lips and held her to him for just a moment. It felt wonderful to melt into his arms and relax knowing that he trusted her so much. "Come on, the kitchen will be fine for a few minutes."

Leah took one last look, he was right, and everything was under control. Nothing would go wrong for a few minutes.

In the living room, sitting around the tree were Ester and Jeremiah, and Colin. Just as she was about to sit down, the door opened and Moses came in, shaking the snow off his shirt. "Have I missed anything?" he asked, rushing across to warm himself by the fire.

"We're just about to start," Abraham said.

"How is Dinah?" Leah asked, still worried despite the fact that she had seen her at the service.

Moses blushed and looked down at his hands. "I think that Uri will have something to tell you tomorrow, but I'm not entirely sure. However, Conrad is not well enough to travel, but Dinah and Uri looked very happy when I left. They sent Christmas wishes."

"Well, I can't wait any longer," Jeremiah said. "Merry Christmas everybody. Now, my first gift will be to my beautiful *fraa*." He nodded his head to Abraham and followed him out of the room. A few moments later they came back in carrying the crib covered in a white blanket.

"This is for you, my darling," Jeremiah said as he whipped off the blanket.

Ester's eyes opened wide with joy as she looked upon the beautifully carved and finished crib. It was varnished to show the knots and lines in the wood and the carving was absolutely gorgeous. In the middle of the headboard was a circle awaiting a name to be carved in it. "This is just so... so wonderful," Ester said as she pulled him into her arms. "It pales in comparison to what I got you," she said as she handed him a packet.

Jeremiah opened it, and it looked like a normal Journal but his eyes opened wide with delight. She had bought him a farm journal that she had seen him looking at. It was leather bound and more expensive than they would normally have spent but she knew he would enjoy many hours filling it in and documenting the seasons, the yields, the good times, and the bad. He pulled her to him and kissed her on the forehead. "You know me too well, I love it."

The door opened once more and they all looked up to see Betsy coming in carrying a huge bag. "I'm sorry, have I disturbed you?" she asked making sure she avoided Moses's eyes.

"Of course not, you are very welcome," Ester said and patted the seat next to her.

Betsy took her place and handed out her own gifts. There were small gifts for most of the family but in the bottom of the bag, she pulled out a large parcel and went over to Moses.

"Ester told me that you needed a new quilt. I made this one," she said without looking him in the eyes.

Moses took it with shaking hands and unwrapped the paper to reveal a magnificent quilt of all shades of green. "It is truly beautiful," he said. "*Denke, denke* so much. I bought you this, but it is poor in comparison." He handed her a wrapped gift.

She smiled at him but quickly looked away. Opening the gift, she found a beautiful polished box for recipe cards. It was perfect, exactly what she wanted and it brought a smile to her face. For a moment, she met his eyes. Only, confusion crossed her face. "I love it," she said, "*denke*. Now, I should help Leah."

The rest of the family exchanged gifts of gloves and socks and hats, board games, and more. Leah received a wonderful box of chocolates from the fancy store in

Bird-in-Hand from Abraham. She was delighted with it, as he was, with the soft leather gloves that she gave him.

With that done, Colin made his way across to Moses. "I'm pleased to hear that Uri and Dinah are finally together."

"As am I, brother." Moses glanced across the room at Betsy, but she would not return his gaze and he couldn't help but feel that she was desperately sad.

"Do not worry, I will sort this out for you," Colin said.

"I don't know, maybe we best leave it."

"Do you really like her?" Colin asked.

"I do, but I can't make her like me." With that Moses walked away and Colin realized that he had caused a lot of trouble. Moses was suffering, Betsy was suffering and he had to do something about it. But what, and when could he do it? Christmas was almost over, he hated Betsy to be sad and alone at this time of year. What had he done?

CHAPTER TWENTY-EIGHT

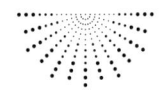

Colin looked across the kitchen and felt a big smile come across his face. So much had changed since he had returned home and he was grateful for all of it, well, most of it. But he had to celebrate the blessings he had.

Jeremiah and Ester were delightfully happy, whispering together, their smiles lighting up their faces. Leah was still bustling around the table, making sure that everyone had eaten their fill. Her meal had been magnificent, a real celebration. He doubted anyone would be able to eat for at least a week!

Abraham could hardly take his eyes off his new *fraa*. The love in them was clear for all to see as was the joy. Colin didn't think he had ever seen his brother so happy.

However, when he looked at Moses and at Betsy, he realized that not everything had gone to plan.

"Why don't you all go into the living room," Leah said. "I will bring some coffee through soon."

"We should help you," Ester said, there is much to do."

"I wouldn't hear of it, go, now!" Leah had her hands on her hips and was giving them a mock stern expression.

"When she uses that look, you'd better obey," Abraham said and he began to hustle people out of the room.

Colin allowed himself to be moved, but he noticed that his brother went back to help Leah as soon as the rest of them were gone.

Betsy was sitting to one side. Her head down, though she was trying to hide her sadness it was clear to all. Moses had retired to his room, also unhappy.

Colin walked across and sat down next to Betsy. "I think I made a mess of things," he said.

But she looked up as if she had hardly heard him and blinked a little. "It has been a lovely day," she said.

"I need to explain something to you," Colin said and was pleased when she put her attention on him. "I love all my brothers and I could see that Uri wanted to court Dinah but couldn't pluck up the courage to say anything. Because of this, I persuaded Moses to spend some time with Dinah. Not to court her, but to explain to her how much Uri liked her."

"I don't understand?" Betsy said.

"I was a meddlesome fool," Colin said and chuckled. "And it didn't go down too well. We told Dinah that Uri likes to walk in the morning, and in that way, we got them together. However, when Uri found out... well, let's just say it did not go down well. I thought I had messed things up and I felt so awful."

"I don't understand why you're telling me this," Betsy said.

"I'm telling you because Moses only has eyes for you. He has ever since he met you, and I know that the two of you could be very happy together. I understand that my blundering foolishness has caused problems and I am really sorry for that. Please, give my brother a second chance."

Betsy let out a sigh. "*Denke* for telling me this but you have to understand that I am much older than your brother. He may have a brief attraction for me, but that will fade. Come the New Year, his sweetness would be gone and reality would set in. I do not wish to put myself through that. I have lost love before, and I do not wish to lose it again. However, *denke*, this has made me feel much better and I promise to enjoy the rest of the day."

"I am so sorry I caused such heartache when all I wanted to do was bring happiness."

Betsy reached out and touched his arm. "*Nee*, you did not. You have a *gut* heart and it is great to have you back here. Do not worry, this is not your fault. Now, I'm going to go help, Leah. She has worked so hard and should not be left to clear up alone."

Colin watched her walk away and couldn't help but feel awful. What trouble he had caused!

* * *

Dinah looked around the table and felt her heart soar. The turkey and vegetables that Uri had brought them, along with the decorations had made this the best Christmas she could remember.

The food was finished, coffee had been served, and they were now just relaxing and enjoying the time together.

Her *daed* looked much stronger and the smile on his face filled her with joy.

"I say it again, *denke*, Uri, for coming to our aid," Conrad said. "You turned up just at the right moment, both my daughter and I are grateful for your company."

"*Ack*, it was nothing. Dinah had the matter under control. And, it was well worth it for this wonderful meal."

"*Nee*, I am very grateful to you for coming to help. For all you have done for us today, and for your company. Let us go through to the other room," Conrad said. "I have a surprise for you both."

Uri and Dinah shared a smile before getting up and pushing him through to his place next to the fire.

"In the cupboard, behind you," Conrad said.

Dinah went to the cupboard and opened the door to find two parcels in there. How had he managed this?

"They are labeled, one for each of you," Conrad said.

Dinah was shocked, how could he have done this? When did he have the time and who would help him? Had it been Bishop Beiler or perhaps Moses? Maybe both? Her stomach churned for she had not told him she was to be married, how would he feel about that? Would it spoil things? Though she knew it was what he wanted, had he expected it so soon? Their life would change so much, was he ready for it?

With a huge smile on her face, Dinah passed one of the parcels to Uri and took the other herself. Slowly, she opened it and her face lit up with joy. It was a new clock for the kitchen, a singing bird clock and it was beautiful. How had he managed this? "*Denke,* this is absolutely wonderful, *denke, denke.*"

"Your turn now, young man. I'm hoping you might give me some news in a few months that will make me very happy," Conrad said to Uri. "Maybe, even sooner, I do not mind!"

Uri's cheeks flushed a bright red and he looked down at the package and began to open it. It was an insulated lunch pack and he grinned with delight. "This will be perfect for when I'm out watching the birds. It looks like it's big enough for two. *Denke.* I have something for both of you as well." He brought out a bag of his own and passed a large flat parcel to Conrad.

"*Ack,* I hope I know what this is." With eager hands, he tore off the wrapping to reveal the box beneath. It was the board game, Farmopoly. "*Denke,* we will have many happy hours with this. It is perfect."

Uri smiled but he looked insecure and pulled out another parcel. "When I made this, I thought it was perfect," he said. "However, now, I realize that it is not the sort of thing that a woman would want. I am sorry. Sometimes, we men are not that clever."

"Do not be so silly," Dinah said and took the parcel from him. She opened it with shaking hands and was delighted to see an almost perfect carving of a Wigeon. The birds they had seen together, that day by the river. "It is beautiful," she said. "I love it. *Denke, denke* so much."

Dinah passed out her gifts, a quilt for her *daed*, which would keep his knees warm while he was in his chair, and a pair of soft leather gloves for Uri. Though both were received with love and joy; she felt she had not done as well as the men. But it didn't matter. She could see the joy on both of their faces. This was the spirit of Christmas.

"Do you have anything to say?" Conrad asked.

Dinah shook her head. They had given their thanks, what more did he want? Now, she noticed that he was looking at Uri.

"Can I tell him?" Uri asked.

Dinah blushed, it was all so sudden and yet, her heart was sure. She knew this was what she wanted, so she nodded.

"If I have your permission, I would like to marry your daughter," Uri said.

"You have my permission and my blessing," Conrad said. "You have made an old man very happy. I knew this was happening. I've seen men bursting with happiness before along with the slight looks that flashed in my direction. You were wondering, will the *daed* approve? I'm right, aren't I, that is what you have been thinking."

"You are. *Denke*, I can't wait to join the family."

"I know it is not supposed to be, but you can kiss. After all, there is mistletoe by the window."

Dinah felt her heart stutter. But Uri pulled her into his arms and kissed her beneath the window. She melted into his arms and felt all the joy of the season as his lips touched hers. As they pulled away, a shadow moved outside. Was someone there?

* * *

Colin took a step back from the window as Dinah and Uri noticed him. The last thing he wanted was to shock them, but the grin on his face was huge. At least one of his brothers was happy, and it looked like this whole family was happy. It felt *gut* to have at least helped Uri.

Turning, he made his way back through the snow. There was no point in disturbing them more.

A noise had him turning and he looked over to see the door to the little property opening. Uri popped his head out. "Where do you think you're going? Come on in here, and get warm."

Colin grinned and turned back, trudging through the snow to the house. He kicked it off his boots before going in and taking off his hat. "Conrad, Diana, I hope you have had a great Christmas."

"It has been the best I can remember," Conrad said with a big smile on his face. "It is *gut* to see you back with us."

"*Denke*, it is *gut* to be back."

"Can I get you a coffee or a bite to eat?" Dinah asked.

"*Nee*, I will just take a moment by the fire, that would be great," Colin said.

"How did Leah's meal go?" Dinah asked.

"It was perfect," Colin said. "I think she will be here to see you tomorrow, I will not tell her your news unless you want me to?"

Uri was standing next to Dinah and he pointed to Colin to take a seat. Dinah and Uri sat down next to each other and Colin sat opposite so they were all in a circle with Conrad close to the fire.

"What news?" Uri asked with a chuckle.

"You may as well tell him," Dinah said, "after all, he did have a hand in this."

Uri put his arm around Dinah and kissed her forehead. "*Ack*, I think you are right." Uri turned to his brother with a huge smile on his face. "Dinah and I are to be married."

Colin let out a gasp of joy. "That is fabulous. At least I didn't mess everything up."

"You didn't mess things up at all, I see into your heart and I see a *gut* man," Dinah said.

Colin nodded. "You are too kind. But I fear that the harm I have done to Moses and Betsy cannot be easily undone."

"With faith and prayer, all things can change," Conrad said.

"You are very kind. But I made a mess of things. I almost destroyed it for you too, I have made things very difficult for Moses. I do not know what is to happen, I do not know how I can help."

"Do not worry, Colin," Dinah said. "This year is nearly over; the year ahead is like a bird poised for flight. It is ready to take wing and soar into the skies. It is full of possibilities and full of hope and if we all stick together as a family, we can get through anything. This misunderstanding will be forgotten by next Christmas. But I have to ask, you worry about others, what about yourself? Will you ever find love?"

Colin's face glowed as red as the coals in the fire. "I think I need to worry about Moses before I worry about myself."

"Maybe, but do not deny yourself love." Dinah looked up at Uri and a smile on her face said everything. "It is the most wonderful thing, it fills the heart with joy, and makes you realize that you can do anything, face anything and that there is always hope. This has been the best Christmas I can ever remember."

The sentiment was echoed around the room. Everyone was enjoying Christmas and they had faith that tomorrow would be a *gut* day.

If you missed it grab book 1 here

THE AMISH LANDSCAPE – PREVIEW

The wind lifted the ties of Emma's kapp and let them drift across her face. The breeze was nice, refreshing, and gave her a sense of freedom as did the open view before her. There was still a chill in the air and spring was yet to bring the hedges to life, but she loved this time of year.

Behind her was the center of Faith's Creek and she could still smell the enticing smells from the bakery. To her side was a cup of coffee and a raspberry and white chocolate muffin nibbled on but almost forgotten. In front of her was the widest part of the creek, or river, that the district was famous for. The sky above was blue, the blue so deep and perfect it made you feel small. It gave you a sense of the wonder of *Gott's* world, of the magnificence in the smallest things that could be taken for granted if you let them pass. The occasional cloud drifted across in front of her. They seemed lazy and indulgent, not quite as fluffy as the cumulus clouds of summer but still, they lifted her spirits. What would it be like to fly high like a cloud?

Emma chuckled, her sister Susan would consider such thoughts wasteful, "How will that get you a husband?" She could almost hear the stern tone in her voice. Lifting her paintbrush she let it slide across the paper and as if by magic the cloud was now immortalized in front of her.

Normally when she painted, she liked to work somewhere more remote. Tonight she only had time to walk here if she was to get any painting done. She had left her work in the clothing factory, ridden her bike back to Faith's Creek, and grabbed a sandwich and two muffins before sitting down to paint. Maybe two was too many, what would Susan say? That reminded her of the muffin and she lifted it and took a bite but her eyes were pulled back to the scene and how best to bring it to life on the paper before her.

The other side of the creek was pastureland and grazing on it were two large Belgian draft horses. The animals seemed to capture the sunlight and it enhanced the dapples on their chestnut coats and made their flaxen manes and tails shine.

It was Emma's second day on this painting and even though the horses had moved she had already penciled them in. All she needed to do now was capture the magnificence and the glory that embodied the horse's spirit. Holding her breath, she dipped her brush into the water and then back to the pallet, picking both orange and brown she mixed them together and delicately applied them to the paper. It was perfect, the brush glided from her hands bringing the horses to life.

Emma took another bite of the muffin as she studied the horses and their muscles. She had it, and still with the muffin in her left hand, she bent back to the painting.

Every now and then, she could hear voices behind her but one particular voice made her brush freeze above the paper. It was Amity Wayne. Emma bit back a groan. Amity was well known as a bitter old woman, a gossip, and someone who liked to pull others down.

"No wonder she's so fat," Amity said not caring that her voice carried.

Emma could not see who she was talking to and whoever it was, they were good enough to keep their reply to a whisper.

"Mark my words," Amity said again, "I don't think it's right. It goes against the Ordnung. I shall be talking to the bishop. Vanity and frivolity that's all it is, there should be no vanity in our district."

"I agree with you," another voice said.

The brush was shaking in Emma's hand. Yes, she was a little large, but surely that was the way *Gott* made her? It didn't matter. Cruel remarks had been part of her life for as long as she could remember. Emma Byler, 37 and still unmarried. 37 and hardly been courted. The woman could lose her home because she hadn't bothered to get a husband. The woman who wasted her time painting when there was work to be done. Who would even look at her! She had heard it all and even though she pretended she was strong, that she didn't care, it still cut her to the bone.

Biting back her tears she added more paint to her brush, but as she touched the paper her hand shook so badly that it smudged. The painting was ruined.

Rinsing her brush once more she wiped it clean and packed away her things. Luckily, her journey home would be in the opposite direction to Amity. Hopefully, they wouldn't meet.

With her paints, brushes, and easel all gathered under her arms, Emma started on her walk home. Even though she knew it was silly, she couldn't help but let a tear fall. Her work in the *Englischer* factory was hard, but it kept a roof over her head, just, and gave her enough money to spend on her painting supplies. Though there had always been a few mumblings about her paintings — until her *daed's* death — no one had said it out loud. Marlin Byler was a jolly man, even after his stroke. A good man who loved his community, but would not hear a bad word about his daughters.

Emma guessed that it was fine to have a little frivolity when you were looking after a dying relative. For a moment she was angry and feelings of pity overwhelmed her. Her sisters had it so easy. They were much younger than her and yet both were married. Susan had a three-year-old, little Dan. Mary had been married a few years now but so far had no children. Sometimes that worried Emma but her sister had not spoken about it.

Emma whispered a prayer of gratitude. Even though her *mamm* had been ill since Mary, her youngest sister, was born, they had had a good life. Emma had raised the two sisters and helped her *daed* as much as she could. It left little time to court and though she had always been happy, Emma had turned a little bit to food for comfort. Caring was hard work for a young girl and yet she wouldn't have missed it for the world. The hours she had with her *mamm* were treasured.

Emma walked past a large hedge up to a crossroads, struggling to carry all of her equipment and deep in thought. *What would she do if she lost her job?* Without looking she stepped out and was so engrossed that she didn't notice the buggy trotting towards her.

"Whoa!" A deep voice called.

The sound of hooves clattering to a halt sent a shock that jolted her heart and tingled all down her arms. Emma looked up to see the horse almost on top of her. She stepped aside quickly but dropped her easel and watercolor pad onto the track. For one awful moment, she thought the horse and wheels of the buggy would go straight over it. However, the buggy was expertly steered around it and pulled to a halt.

Emma dropped to her knees to gather up her supplies. Could this day get any worse?

※ ※ ※

Jesse King looked out over the horse's ears as it trotted along the country lane. Faith's Creek was everything he could've hoped for and he knew that within a short time he would have more customers than he could manage. The local Bishop, Amos Beiler had invited him here as the previous blacksmith had retired. In his Ohio community, his brothers ran their family blacksmith and Jesse, even though welcome, had been looking for a new start. It was just a few years since his parents had passed, within a few months of each other. It seemed that their love was so strong that one could not survive without the other.

Shortly after that, the woman he had been courting had left him for a better prospect. It broke his heart and left him bitter and he had not approached a woman since. Although he knew that Rebecca's Zook did not deserve his love, she had it, and though he had now left her behind, his heart was still broken. It felt like a wizened old walnut to him. Hard and impenetrable.

It was at that time that he started to wonder about leaving his home. The memories were bad enough, seeing Rebecca married to Aaron Wagler was hard, but the hardest thing was the sympathy. Although he loved his aunts and uncles and brothers and their wives they were constantly plying him with sympathy. Either that or they were offering up alternatives. Jesse was not ready to give his heart again and he wondered if he ever would be.

Over the top of the hedge, he could see a young woman walking up to the crossroads. Her head was bowed and she seemed to be carrying a heavy load, both physically and metaphorically. As the horse approached the corner he waved to her but she did not look up. A hand clutched onto his heart as he realized she hadn't seen or heard him and she walked straight out almost under the horse's hooves.

"Whoa!" he shouted, hauling on the reins and steering the horse to the side. The woman raised her head and dropped all she was carrying. Jesse pulled the horse to a halt and jumped down. How could he have been so silly? He nearly ran her over!

The woman had dropped to her knees and was busily gathering up her things. Though she was dressed in the traditional Amish garb with a kapp, a dark blue dress, and a white apron. He could see that she had dropped what looked like art supplies.

The words of Bishop Bender were harsh in his ears. "Frivolity and wasteful time will not be tolerated. Work, young man, work and prayer, that is our way." He had heard them many times in his youth when he used to sketch. That was when he realized he hadn't picked up a pencil to do anything other than work in many years.

"Here, let me help you," he said bending to his knees.

She seemed oblivious and he reached out to grab her pallet of paints and at the same time she reached out too. Their hands touched and she turned to him and he saw the most beautiful pale blue eyes he had ever seen. There was something in them that pulled at his heart, was it the deep sadness, or was it something else?

Jesse felt his cheeks color and pulled his hand away as if it was burned. This was ridiculous. He was a man of 40. There was no way a woman should make him blush but there was something about her. She was beautiful and curvy with a face that looked worried and was damp with tears when he imagined it would bring out the sunshine if she smiled.

"I'm so sorry," he said. "Let me help you."

Of course, she must be married, she was beautiful and maybe a few years younger than him. Quickly he pushed away the feeling that this meeting was meant to be and tried to help. How would it look if the first week in his new district he upset one of its members?

She nodded her head and bowed so he could not see her face. Jesse wanted to comfort her but instead, he picked up her pad. It had opened to a watercolor of a small copse of trees not far from here. Cattle grazed in front of it and a bird sat on the hedge. It was so real, so beautiful that he wanted to touch it and he knew that his jaw had dropped open. "Did you paint this?" he asked.

The woman stood up and folded her arms. "I don't need you telling me I shouldn't be wasting my time," she said and grabbed the pad before turning and walking away, her arms overloaded.

Find out if Emma and Jesse can overcome their difficulties in The Amish Landscape.

ALSO BY SARAH MILLER

All my books are FREE on Kindle Unlimited

If you love Amish Romance, the sweet, clean stories of Sarah Miller receive free stories and join me for the latest news on upcoming books here

These are some of my reader favorites:

The Amish Faith and Family Collection

A New Amish Love

A Return to Faith

15 Tales of Amish Love and Grace

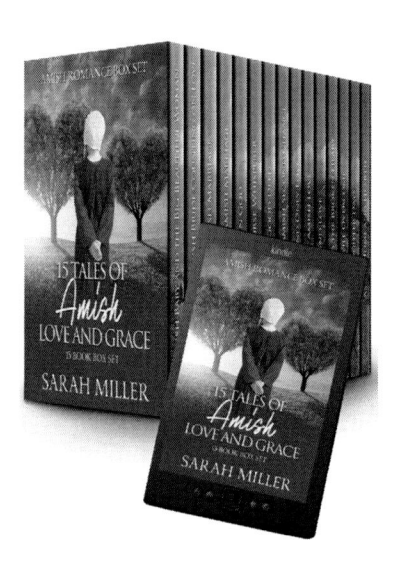

Find all Sarah's books on Amazon and click the yellow follow button

+ Follow

This book is dedicated to the wonderful Amish people and the faithful life that they live.

Go in peace, my friends.

As an independent author, Sarah relies on your support. If you enjoyed this book, please leave a review on Amazon or Goodreads.

ABOUT THE AUTHOR

Sarah Miller was born in Pennsylvania and spent her childhood close to the Amish people. Weekends were spent doing chores; quilting or eventually babysitting in the community. She grew up to love their culture and the simple lifestyle and had many Amish friends. The one thing that you can guarantee when you are near the Amish, Sarah believes is that you will feel close to God.

Many years later she married Martin who is the love of her life and moved to England. There she started to write stories about the Amish. Recently after a lot of persuasion from her best friend she has decided to publish her stories. They draw on inspiration from her relationship with the Amish and with God and she hopes you enjoy reading them as much as she did writing them. Many of the stories are based on true events but names have been changed and even though they are authentic at times artistic license has been used.

Sarah likes her stories simple and to hold a message and they help bring her closer to her faith. She currently lives in Yorkshire, England with her husband Martin and seven very spoiled chickens.

She would love to meet you on Facebook at https://www.facebook.com/SarahMillerBooks

Sarah hopes her stories will both entertain and inspire and she wishes that you go with God.

©Copyright 2022 Sarah Miller
All Rights Reserved
Sarah Miller

License Notes
This e-Book may not be resold. Your continued respect for author's rights is appreciated.

This story is a work of fiction; any resemblance to people is purely coincidence. All places, names, events, businesses, etc. are used in a fictional manner. All characters are from the imagination of the author.

Manufactured by Amazon.ca
Acheson, AB